HEARTBREAKER

GAMEBREAKERS #2

KAT MIZERA
ELISE FABER

GAMEBREAKERS

Icebreaker
Heartbreaker
Dealbreaker
Rulebreaker
Oathbreaker

CHAPTER ONE

Royal

I FUCKING HATE THIS SHIT.

The cameras. The lights. The vapid, plastic celebrities surrounding me on all sides.

It's fake as shit.

Always.

"Smile," Briar, my little sister in all but blood, orders from next to me. "The camera's on you."

"Fuck the cameras," I mutter, but I do it from between gritted teeth that are exposed because I've forced my mouth into some semblance of a smile.

It feels rusty. Unused.

Because I haven't had much to smile about over the last couple of years.

"Play the game and they go away," she says, leaning close and speaking into my ear so that no TikTokkers can play Read Our Lips later today. "You know that I'm right."

I do.

Hence the reason I'm fucking smiling.

Hence the reason I'm fucking *here* in the first place.

A godawful way to spend an evening—sitting in uncomfortable chairs while listening to badly produced musical numbers, a host who's desperate to be funny but is only cringeworthy, and people with far too much power getting thanked for doing nothing.

I grind my teeth together.

Because *I'm* the one who's doing nothing now.

Ever since the accident—

"And the winner for Song of the Year is…"

"Here we go!" Briar says, taking my hand—my fucking *hand* —and squeezing it.

Even as I process the touch—dulled, wrong—and fight down the urge to recoil from the contact, the presenter continues talking.

"...*Forever in Rewind* by Jade Cantrell!"

The crowd erupts into applause while Briar squeals and leans into me, "You did it!"

Surreptitiously, I pull my hand from hers, nod at the stage. "No. *She* did it."

The tiny slip of a woman in a huge, sparkling ball gown who's hugging someone next to her then standing. The beautiful female who's somehow gracefully ascending the stairs that lead up to the stage despite the miles and miles of fabric that are practically dwarfing her petite frame.

Jade Cantrell.

A small-town country girl who was making a name for herself in Nashville—

At least until the surprise genre-bending crossover hit (that I wrote) topped the Billboard charts and propelled her into worldwide stardom.

And Jade became the biggest musical act in the world right now.

Selling out stadiums.

A huge international tour that sold out in seconds.

And now…

Song of the Year.

The applause begins to die down—though, in fairness, the tepid congratulations from her contemporaries is drowned out by the audience in the balcony behind us, so really, it's her fans that are quieting.

Because she's approaching the microphone.

Opening her mouth.

And—

Lightning shoots through my veins.

I've heard the song—of course I have. I wrote it. I came up with the melodies. I recorded it. And then I sent it off to be made into magic. And even then, I heard advance copies, made suggestions for tweaks and additions on the production side, listened to it dozens, if not hundreds of times.

But when Jade Cantrell begins talking into that microphone, when her melodic voice echoes out of the huge speakers mounted above the stage, the room fills with…

Music.

Fucking beautiful music that hits me in my soul.

Hard.

I'm frozen into place, watching each minute movement she makes as she adjusts the microphone, smiles, and continues to speak.

Because I haven't felt like this since…

I had two hands that functioned and I could make music the way I wanted.

It's captivating. It's the *je ne sais quoi* every musician wishes they had. It's…magic.

And—

"She's got it," Briar whispers, her shoulder pressing against mine. "That spark that makes the whole world sit up and pay attention to her."

I nod.

But don't look at my sister because I'm still paying attention to Jade's every word as she thanks her family, her friends, her music teacher, her agent and publicist and assistant. All the usual bullshit.

But done in a way that's effortless and a pleasure to listen to and doesn't come across as fake or insincere.

Yup.

She's fucking *got* it.

"Without Grandma Louise, I never would have been here." Her throat works, emotion shimmering through her words. "Thank you for believing in me when I didn't."

Christ.

That even makes *me* feel something.

Clearly, it's been too long since I've gotten laid.

Lost in the pleasure of female curves.

Out of my head so I'm not constantly thinking about—

"Ready to go?" I mutter to Briar, leaning forward, preparing to stand up and get the hell out of here.

Away from the cameras and the uninspiring, selfish A-listers.

Away from the voice that seems to reach right into my chest and claws at my heart, my soul.

Away from the eyes that come to me as I hear—

"And thank you to Royal Ewing, who wrote this beautiful song for me and helped me transform it into something extraordinary."

I jerk, mid-rise from my seat, distantly tracking the gazes turning in my direction, the cameras doing a quick pivot, the attention…

Settling square onto me.

Panic dislodges the bewitching voice, digging deeper, slicing my insides to ribbons.

It's hard to breathe, to think, to—

Briar settles her hand on my leg.

"Smile," she orders softly, leaning in and waving at the camera positioned what feels like all of three inches away from my face.

I do something that *might* approximate a smile.

"This is for you," Jade says and my gaze jerks back to the tiny, sparkle-covered woman. I see her lift the award in my direction for a moment before she smiles, waves, and turns to exit the stage, disappearing between the curtains as the music rises to a crescendo and the host steps toward the microphone to send the television broadcast to commercial.

"Get me the fuck out of here," I hiss at Briar, already feeling the walls closing in, knowing that people are going to come socialize, going to come ask questions, going to come and try to maneuver favors out of me.

"On it," she says.

And to her credit, she is.

Then again, Briar is one of the most capable people I know.

Certainly more so than a former rock star with a bum hand who's a second away from having a panic attack over something I used to live for, revel in, demand—

Attention.

It's stifling now.

My lungs are struggling to draw in air.

Black intrudes on the edges of my vision.

"Royal!"

Briar grips my arm and hauls me up to my feet, stepping between the man—an agent who I want absolutely nothing to fucking do with—and myself, guiding me to the aisle and out of his slimy, grimy crosshairs.

"Hey, bud, long time no see," says a man I recognize (as in a creep who's trying to make a comeback but seems to be doing his level best to undermine his career with dumbass racist tweets). "Let's chat, huh?"

"Never going to fucking happen," Briar mutters, though her smile stays in place.

Something I track because I'm not looking at the crowd.

Because I'm not looking at the cameras.

My gaze is glued to Briar as she gets me out of the auditorium and into the wings of the theater.

"Stay there," she whispers, tucking me into a shadowy alcove, my body almost completely hidden behind a billowing navy velvet curtain.

"Bri—"

A squeeze of my shoulder. "I'll be right back."

Panic makes me want to shake my head, to yank her back against me and hold tight until everything inside me calms—

But I'm not a fucking pussy, okay?

I shove that down, slap a lid on it.

"I'm fine," I rasp, not sounding the least bit *fine*.

"Of course you are," she says, not calling me on my bullshit. Another squeeze before she drops her hand. "I'll be right back."

I nod.

Her expression is far too gentle for my comfort but I don't have to sit in that because then she's disappearing down the hall, leaving me in the shadows, the rest of the world moving around me.

That's a familiar feeling, and it settles me until she comes back a couple of minutes later and guides me down a narrow, dimly lit hallway.

"Where are we going?" Okay, that sounds less *settled* and more…hanging on by a thread.

"Somewhere quiet," she says, thankfully ignoring my tone as she leads me into a nondescript green room and closes the door behind us. There's a mirror surrounded with lights, a vanity for makeup, a couch on the far wall, and a table loaded with snacks plunked in front of it. "I got the all-clear to put you here for a few minutes," Briar explains. "You'll be left alone while I call Quentin"—my head of security—"and get your car pulled around."

"Thanks, Thorny," I tell her.

A light swat to my chest in response to the nickname before she says quietly, "Being helpful is what I do best."

"You're more than just that."

She gives a soft shake of her head, always discounting

herself, never seeing how fucking great she is, but I know now's not the time to try to change her mind.

I need to get the fuck out of here before I have a full-blown panic attack in front of these assholes.

"Sit tight," she orders softly.

I nod, drop onto the couch. "Sitting."

Her mouth twitches.

Then she's gone, the door *clicking* closed softly behind her.

I exhale, rolling my shoulders, my neck, willing the rest of the tension to just go the fuck away.

This time, thankfully, as the seconds pass, those twisted emotions inside me loosen their vice-like grip on my insides and begin to fade away.

So much so, that I feel almost normal by the time the handle turns less than three minutes later, the door swinging inward.

"That was fast," I start to say, anticipating the red flash of Briar's hair.

Instead, I get…

Blond curls.

Miles and miles of sparkle-covered fabric.

Soulful gray eyes.

A tiny country-pop dynamo.

Jade Cantrell freezes in the open door, her mouth dropping open, shock ricocheting across her gorgeous face.

But her surprise only lasts for a moment.

Because then she smiles…

And the bottom falls out of my world.

CHAPTER TWO

Jade

HOLY HOTTER-THAN-THE-SURFACE-OF-MARS-IN-THE-MIDDLE-OF-SUMMER-WITHOUT-SUNSCREEN.

My skin tingles just looking at Royal freakin' Ewing.

I mean, where in the there-are-hot-guys-all-over-Los-Angeles-but-this-one-is-spectacular has he been hiding?

Okay, I know the answer but it's a little hard to think with him just a few feet away from me.

I've been a huge fan for a long time, and have always found him handsome, but nothing prepares me for the hotness he exudes in person. I had no idea he would be here tonight, much less hanging out in my dressing room.

"Hi," I say, when I finally find my voice. "I'm Jade."

"I know." He slowly gets to his feet, eyes locked with mine.

My heart does a little staccato dance in my chest as he approaches me, left hand outstretched. "Royal Ewing."

"Believe me, I know." I put my hand in his and the sparks are so strong I almost jump.

What is happening here?

"Congratulations on Song of the Year."

Our hands linger much longer than is appropriate.

Except I don't want him to stop touching me.

"I couldn't have done it without you."

A lazy shrug. "I just wrote it—you made the song come alive."

Deep blue eyes search my face and I'm a little mesmerized.

"Th-thank you."

Finally, I pull my hand from his.

Before I do something stupid.

"I apologize if I'm not supposed to be here." He looks around. "My assistant said she got permission for me to sit in here while we wait for our car to come around."

"Oh, it's fine." I wave a hand. "I wasn't planning to come back here but my limo's stuck in traffic and I wanted to powder my nose."

"If you'd rather I leave..." His voice trails and I quickly shake my head.

"Not at all. Make yourself comfortable." I move to the small dressing table and plop down on the stool. Well, as much as someone wearing a full hoop skirt can plop. What was I thinking, wearing this contraption? My agent thought it would be elegant and classy, which it is, but it's uncomfortable. I have to pee but there's no way I can get to the bathroom by myself.

I open my tiny evening bag and pull out some lip gloss. My lipstick stain has held up well but my lips are a little dry so I dab on the gloss and pucker in the mirror. Tall, dark, and ridiculously hot is watching, but I don't care.

I'm excited to simply bask in his presence.

Royal Ewing is a legend.

One of the most talented guitarists in rock and roll.

Well, he was.

Until a car accident robbed him of the use of his right hand.

My heart breaks for him every time I read something about the accident, and I notice that his right arm hangs limply at his side. I can't help but wonder if it hurts. If he spends all day everyday thinking about the fact that he'll never play guitar again.

His accident was big news when it happened, the gory details all over the media.

Then his divorce had been so ugly, and so very public.

I can't imagine what he went through.

We've never met but I feel for him every time I read another news article about him.

Now he's in my dressing room.

And even more intoxicating than I imagined.

I catch his eye in the mirror and he is, indeed, watching me, as if he's reading my mind.

A warm flush covers my body.

Not because I'm embarrassed or doing anything wrong, but because his gaze is dark, penetrating, almost as titillating as his touch was.

And I'm completely under a spell.

"Are you going to any after parties?" I ask, desperate for some semblance of normal conversation.

"No." He pauses. "You?"

"My producer, Rico Galagos, is having a small get-together at his place, so I'll head over there for a while. After I change out of this dress. I don't know what I was thinking wearing something I can barely move in."

"You look beautiful." His voice is deep and it sends shivers down my spine.

"Thank you." I turn, cocking my head slightly. "If I'd known you were going to be here, I would have brought you on stage with me."

His brows furrow. "I'm glad you didn't. I prefer to stay out of the spotlight."

"Why?" The word pops out before I can stop it, and I immediately back pedal. "I'm sorry. That's none of my business."

"It's all right." He leans against the door. "I just get tired of the Hollywood bullshit sometimes. It's all so fake."

"But you came tonight."

"I knew you were going to win," he says softly, "and I wanted to be here for it."

"Well, I appreciate that. I'm so glad we got to meet. Our song changed my career—my life. It's been the craziest year."

"Good crazy or bad crazy?"

"A little of both, to be honest. There's been a lot of good. Money, success, an incredible tour, TV shows, interviews—all the things we dream of before we're successful. But the down side is…the constant attention. The lack of privacy. I can't even relax at home now because the press is camped outside twenty-four seven."

"Wherever you're living when you hit it big," he says quietly, "has to become your former residence. Or a secondary residence. You have to move or they'll never give you any peace."

I haven't even considered selling my Nashville farmhouse. "But I love my home."

"You'll love the newer, bigger, more private house just as much," he says drolly.

"I go to my farm to unwind, relax, write songs…"

"How's that working out for you now that you're famous?"

I chuckle. "Not that well, I guess."

"Would you like a little unsolicited advice?" he asks as he strolls toward me.

"Absolutely."

He stops in front of me, his body mere inches from mine, his voice soft when he says, "Surround yourself with people you trust. *Really* trust. Not just the people who got you where you are—because they don't always have your best interests at heart—but honest-to-goodness smart, loyal people who will put your career, and your needs, first."

"How do you know who those people are?" I ask just as softly. "Sometimes it's hard to tell the good from the bad."

"And it'll only get harder from here on out. That's why the people you surround yourself with are so important. There's a price to pay for each level of success. And the more successful you are, the higher the price."

"Why does that sound ominous?"

He shrugs. "It can be. Like I said, get the right team around you. That's the only way to navigate it."

"There are a lot of moving parts in my career right now, and it's probably only going to get worse after tonight. I trust my team, but I'm not really close to any of them. If that makes sense? From where I'm sitting, I don't think they put my needs first. I'm just a name on a talent roster to them."

"That's going to change after tonight," he says. "Make sure you don't reward them for mediocre effort."

"That sounds great in theory, but how do you put that into practice? Because the reality is, I've had this team since I got my first record deal. Now, I win this big award and I suddenly dump everyone? How does that make me look?"

He takes my hand in his, squeezes lightly. "Like a smart, successful young woman taking control of her career and doing what's best for her future."

"Is that what you did?" I ask quietly.

He pauses and then shakes his head. "No. I didn't. And that's why I'm giving you the benefit of my experience. I was stupid. And now I'm paying the price. But that's another story for another night."

"Maybe you'll tell me someday."

A long moment of silence falls between us.

"Maybe I will," he finally says, voice quiet, the words gentle fingers stroking along the bare skin of my wrist.

Our eyes are glued together, as if neither of us can look away.

And I really don't want to.

He's enigmatic, gorgeous, mysterious, and the complete opposite of the kind of guys I usually go for. Standing here in this little dressing room, it feels like the outside world doesn't exist. It's just us. And I can't explain why I'm so drawn to him.

The way he's looking at me—like a starving man about to have his first meal in a long time—I know he feels it too.

I just don't know what to do about it.

Any minute now, my assistant Rosie is going to come in and tell me the limo is here.

Royal will most likely be heading to his ride as well.

If I don't say or do something to prolong our time together, I may never see him again.

And for some reason, I'm not okay with that.

"Come to Rico's party with me," I blurt out. "I'd like to talk to you some more. I have so many questions..."

He looks away, his eyes suddenly hooded. "I don't do parties."

"Rico has the guest list locked down. No cameras, no press, just a group of close friends and their dates. I—" I nibble at my bottom lip. "Please come with me. I'm not ready to stop talking to you." It feels a little awkward, putting it out there like this, but what choice do I have?

He gives me another of those penetrating stares.

He's thinking about it.

And I'm practically holding my breath.

I'm not usually so bold with men, but there's something about him that makes me want to know more.

"I could come for an hour, I guess," he says in a gruff voice. "I'd like to talk to you more too."

"Jade?" Rosie sticks her head in the door. "There you are. Are you ready to go? Limo's here."

"Yes." I turn to Royal. "Come in my car? My driver can take you home whenever you're ready."

A nod. "I just need to text my assistant to make sure she gets home all right."

"Perfect." I grab my purse and move toward the door as he types into his phone.

Glee fills me and it's all I can do not to skip my way over—well that, *and* the miles and miles of dress weighing me down. It's just…

Holy guacamole.

Royal Ewing is coming to a party.

With *me.*

CHAPTER THREE

Royal

I DON'T LIKE the hungry way her assistant is looking at me as we hurry down the hall, the sparkles from Jade's dress scattering rainbow-filled reflections on the walls as we move.

But I just ignore it as we push out into the night air and quickly move into her car.

My phone buzzes and I glance at the screen as they shut the door behind us.

Rosie says something I can't discern to Jade, but I don't try to eavesdrop as I respond to Briar's message.

Briar: You found someone to fuck when I left you alone for three minutes?

Royal: I'm socializing. Which you wanted. So fuck off.

Royal: And give Tater Tot a hug for me. You know she misses her favorite uncle.

Briar: You're lucky I love you, you giant pain in my ass.

Briar: And, just so you know, I'm telling Frankie you've promised SIX books and just as many songs the next time you put her to bed.

My lips twitch, but I just thumb back a response.

Royal: Make sure Quentin gets you home safe and text me once you're inside and the alarm is set.

Briar: Overprotective, much?

Royal: Dash—or any of the guys—would have my ass if I wasn't.

Briar: *scowly face emoji*

Briar: Try to at least have some fun tonight.

I don't bother to reply to that because fun and Royal Ewing don't go together.

Not any longer, anyway.

My life is brooding, hiding from gossipy assholes, and teaching a three-year-old to play Old MacDonald Has a Farm on a tiny guitar.

If the world could see me now…

The car door opens, and I blink against the flashes of light, shoving my body back into the leather seat, trying to be as inconspicuous as possible.

"Sorry," Jade says a moment later as the door slams closed. "I just needed to let Rosie out so she can head home for the night."

I nod.

The limo moves forward again, inching up and stopping and

then repeating the process many times over as we navigate away from the venue and out onto the city streets.

But it's not until we've hit a good clip on the highway that I realize I should say something.

She's shifting on her seat, gaze pointed out the window as she fusses with that ridiculously large skirt.

"When did you decide you wanted to be a musician?" I ask.

Her eyes—deep gray like thunderstorms—come to mine. "My mom used to say I started singing and dancing in the womb." Her mouth kicks up, and she shifts again. "She teased that I never let her sleep before I was born. Or after," she adds, smile widening, "because I was always learning some instrument or humming a melody or practicing a dance number."

"What did you like to sing?"

Her brows flick up, as though surprised by the question, but then she softens. "Anything, really."

I snort.

She shifts in her seat, one hand on the leather, the other fussing with her skirt. "What?"

"Nothing," I say.

"No, seriously." She shifts again. "What?"

There's a thread of steel in her tone, of annoyance, and I find that intriguing. Definitely intriguing enough to needle at it, just a little bit. "Let me guess," I say dryly. "You were obsessed with boy bands."

Her eyes flick up but she doesn't back down, and I know in an instant that she'll make it, that she'll survive the sharks in this industry, that she'll keep that special brand of magical lightning bottled up inside her instead of allowing it to fade away like so many others have.

"I liked boy bands—or *like*," she corrects. "But I also love The Beatles and the Stones and Nirvana and Dolly and Lady Gaga and Loretta. I'm obsessed with all things Taylor and P!nk and can belt out a Journey or Bon Jovi rock anthem. Maren Morris is incredible and I couldn't have survived my teenage years without Reba or Faith or LeAnn or Alanis. But I'm just as likely to blast Sabrina or Chappell or Beyoncé as I am to sing along with Bonnie Raitt or Janis Joplin or Joan Jett or Stevie Nicks." She smiles and I see the sparks of joy in her eyes, hear the passion in her words. "And don't even get me started on Tina or Prince or Janet or Lauryn Hill or—" Her cheeks color as her gaze catches mine, and she wriggles in her seat again. "I just love music," she whispers. "Beethoven to whatever's hot on the charts to—" A shrug. "I'm blabbering."

"You're *beautiful,*" I murmur back.

Wide gray eyes, those cheeks turning bright pink. "It's all makeup and tailoring." Her mouth curves, and her smile is rueful. "And a metric ton of shapewear. I meant to change before I left the theater, but I got distracted and—" She winces now, pulling at her skirt.

"That's why you're squirming like you've got ants in your pants?"

Pink turns to red. "I—"

I lean over and touch her cheek, running my fingertips over the flush. "Like I said, you're beautiful, ants in your pants or not. And it's not makeup or shapewear or tailoring."

Her lips part, protest welling up in those storm gray eyes.

But I'm still talking…however ill-advised my next words are. "Do you want me to help you?"

She frowns. "With what?"

"Getting more comfortable."

Her brows shoot up now, almost to her hairline. "I…um, what?"

"That's what the bag is for, right?" I ask, nodding at the garment bag hanging from the handle on the far side of the limo, at the duffle from an expensive name brand sitting on the seat beneath it.

"I—" She turns and looks. "Yes, that's my change of clothes. I

—" A shake of her head, her befuddled eyes coming back to mine. "But—"

Fuck, she's cute with those wide eyes and bright cheeks. "I'll undo your zipper and then turn around," I explain. "Give you some privacy while you put on something more comfortable."

A blink.

Another.

Then, "Really?"

I nod. "Can't have you suffering in that metric ton of shapewear."

She nibbles at her bottom lip then nods. "If you don't mind helping me, that would be great."

Don't mind?

Touching this beautiful woman? Getting close enough to inhale the scent of her perfume? To snag a glimpse of the curves that dress and all that shapewear are hiding and I can only guess at?

In answer, I shift closer.

Wide gray eyes.

Pretty pink lips.

I wonder if she's as pink between her legs, if she'll glisten as prettily as she does in the dress.

"Turn around," I order and if my voice is more rasp than command, Jade doesn't call me on it. She just…

Shifts carefully, sweeping her blond curls forward and over her shoulder, and gives me her back.

She has a small tattoo on her nape, and I find myself leaning in to see what it is.

"A bee?" I ask quietly.

Her shoulders hitch up slightly and then she's turning her head, eyes coming to mine. Her mouth is so close that our lips are almost aligned. I can lean forward a mere inch and taste her.

My cock twitches and I almost do just that.

But then she exhales quietly. "My ranch outside of Nashville is where I grew up. We had all sorts of animals—horses, sheep, cows, pigs, and bees." Her eyes close and her expression is a combination of sad and soft. "After my dad passed, my mom threw her whole life into the farm. And one of those things she obsessively took care of—besides me—was the bees. She used to have hives and they were her babies as much as our horses, Bandit and Gunner." She sighs. "The honey…it was some of the best I ever tasted. She sold it at farmer's markets and online and…she used it to fund the studio time when I recorded my first album."

Fuck, that's sweet.

Enough to make my cold dead heart squeeze.

"After she died, though, I wasn't able to keep it going. I was busy and traveling, trying to make it in the music world and I could never find the right person to take care of them like she did. It's like they knew I wasn't her and—" A shake of her head. "Ignore me."

Never.

"So, the bee's for her?"

Jade nods. "What about your family?"

"Both my parents are gone too."

Her smile is small but filled with empathy. "Then you get it."

What it's like to lose my parents? Yes.

But what it's like to speak of them with the love Jade has in her voice? No. That wasn't my life.

"I'm sorry you lost them."

Her fingers find my hand—the wrong hand—and she squeezes lightly.

Wrong and right.

Dulled and sharp.

I slip my fingers free, motion to her to turn around again so I can unzip her. "How long are you in town?"

She doesn't comment on my obvious change in subject, just faces toward the windows again. "Just a few days," she says. "But I'm back and forth between L.A. and elsewhere often." One delicate shoulder lifts as I find the tab of the zipper and start drawing it down.

It parts effortlessly, the twin halves of material revealing creamy skin and a faint smattering of freckles, and…

"You weren't kidding about the shapewear."

She freezes then giggles, holding the front of her dress as I draw the zipper down, down, down. "I told you," she said. "It's all magic tricks and Spandex."

I grin. "Do you have some doves hiding in there?" I tease. "A scarf that changes color?"

Another giggle. "No."

I release the metal tag and slide back into the other seat, barely resisting the urge to slip my hands into the parted material, to peel away the fabric, to get her naked and see how pink and slick I can make her.

She tosses a glance over her shoulder, and I make a show of turning away. "Don't worry," I tell her. "I won't look."

Her mouth hitches up. "A good man in Hollywood?"

"I wouldn't admit to being good," I say to the sound of rustling, of the garment bag being unzipped. "In fact, I'd say I'm far from it."

Mostly because I'm watching her in the reflection of the window.

Watching as she releases her arms, allows the gown to drop away from her body, to fall to the floor of the car.

My dick does more than twitch when I catch a glimpse of those delicate curves, the ass that screams for a spanking as she squirms out of the shapewear.

And then she's reaching forward, slipping another dress from its hanger in the garment bag, tugging it up her body, covering the temptation of her in pale blue fabric.

"Okay," she says softly.

I turn around. "Want me to do that one up?" I ask gruffly.

Her head tilts to the side, curls fanning out behind her. "What'd you say about not being good again?" A quiet question, but no less pointed. "Because I think there's a nice guy hidden in there."

"You don't know me."

Now her chin comes up.

"Then show me."

CHAPTER FOUR

Jade

ELECTRICITY FILLS the air in the car.

I can't breathe when he looks at me, but I can't look away.

He's mesmerizing, larger than life.

And yet, I sense a touch of vulnerability under the cranky exterior.

Despite what he says, my gut tells me he *is* a good guy. Maybe rough around the edges, and definitely closed off, but there's a gentleman beneath the gruff façade. Of course, there's also a ton of chemistry between us. And no mistaking the fact that he's staring at me like he wants to have me for dessert.

"I'm sure you know my story," he says after a moment.

"I know what the press put out there but I've been around enough to know that's probably only half the truth."

He snorts. "You have no idea."

"Oh, believe me, I'm not untouched by the pitfalls of the media."

Our eyes meet and he nods. "None of us are. But the last two years have been rougher than any other time since I started playing rock and roll."

"I'm sorry." I put a hand on his forearm. "I can't imagine what you've gone through. But we don't have to talk about that unless you want to."

He sighs, is quiet for a long moment then says, so softly I can barely hear it, "Talking about the past just rips the scab off wounds that take a long time to heal."

My heart squeezes. "Then tell me about the present."

His blue eyes gentle. "There isn't a whole lot going on in the present. I have a goddaughter I spend a lot of time with. She's three. Her name is Frankie. Her mom is my best friend's sister, and the dad is a deadbeat, so the four of us—me and my buddies Dash, Banks, and Atlas—have essentially stepped into the role."

"That's wonderful," I say. "So instead of having one not-so-great dad, she's got four amazing uncles. She sounds like a lucky little girl."

The obvious love on his face for his niece has my heart squeezing again. "I'd like to think so. I'm teaching her to play guitar. It's about the cutest thing you'll ever see." He hesitates. "Want to see a video?"

"Absolutely."

He opens his phone and soon I'm laughing along with him as a delightful little girl with dark curls plays 'Old MacDonald' and 'Twinkle, Twinkle Little Star.'

"She's good," I say. "There's a lot of potential there."

"Yeah. She's a natural."

"She reminds me of me. I started young too. And I couldn't get enough. Guitar, piano, saxophone…I even tried the trumpet in marching band in high school."

"That's something I'd pay to see," he says, chuckling.

"It was short-lived, thankfully. I quit after freshman year and joined jazz band instead."

"Sounds better than standing outside in the August heat in Tennessee.'

"You got that right—oh, we're here."

We're pulling through the gate at Rico's house, and there are only a handful of cars outside.

"This is Rico Galagos, right?"

"Yes. Do you know him?"

"Only by reputation. I've never met him."

"He's a good guy. One of those people I think I can trust to be in my inner circle."

"Good to know."

My driver, John, pulls to a stop and then gets out and opens the door for me. He helps me out of the car, and Royal is right behind me. My pulse speeds. I'm acutely aware of his closeness, and I can't help but shiver when he casually puts his hand at the small of my back as we walk toward the entrance.

This is what it feels like to be Royal Ewing's center of attention.

I don't know how long it's going to last, but it's magical. Far beyond anything I could have imagined in my fantasies.

"There she is—the lady of the hour!" Rico is short and slight but what he lacks in physicality he makes up for in personality. He has a loud, booming voice and a huge, infectious smile.

"Congratulations, sweetheart." Rico's husband, Marcel, has a more subdued greeting but pulls me in for a warm hug. "We're so proud of you."

"Thank you." I hug him back. "Guys, this is—"

"Royal Ewing." Rico doesn't hesitate to hold out his hand. "Welcome."

"Thank you for allowing me to be an uninvited guest." Royal is smooth as he shifts the handshake to his left hand—as if he's done this a thousand times—and my heart breaks a little. I don't know the extent of his injury, but from what I've read, they almost had to amputate. He's lucky to have the hand, much less any use of it.

It has to be devastating for a guitar player—one of the best guitarists in the world—to lose not just his ability to play, but his career.

I have so many questions, but he'll tell me when and if he's ready.

I don't want to push him.

"Any time," Rico says. "I'm a big fan." Royal seems at ease now, as if he's attended parties like this a million times.

He probably has.

"Appreciate that."

More introductions are made and then Rico points. "Everyone has gathered out back by the pool. There's food and champagne. We'll do a toast later, but in the meantime, make yourselves at home."

"Thank you." I slide my hand through Royal's left arm and whisper, "I'm starving. I didn't eat all day to make sure I looked as good as possible in that dress."

"Doesn't matter how much you eat—you'd still look drop dead gorgeous no matter what you're wearing."

A flush tinges my skin but a wave of happiness hits me at the same time.

When was the last time I felt so comfortable on a date?

Even if it's not a *real* date, he practically saw me naked in the car.

And as far as I'm concerned, that's close enough.

There's a huge spread of food on a row of tables set up outside, and I sigh happily.

"Shrimp cocktail," I murmur. "And caviar."

"This is quite a feast," Royal says.

I don't know how I'm supposed to deal with the situation with his injured hand, because I notice that he hasn't grabbed a plate, but I figure if I treat it like it's not a big deal then it won't be. I pile some shrimp on my dish and glance at him. "You want to share with me?"

"Sure." He stuffs his hands in his pockets.

I take a little of everything—except the shrimp. I take a lot of that. Then I proffer the dish to Royal. "You carry this while I get us two glasses of champagne."

"Perfect." There are too many emotions lurking in the depths of his blue eyes for me to decipher, but it's hard to miss the gratitude.

We settle on a small loveseat near the fire pit and, once again, I'm keenly aware of his nearness. The warmth of his body next to mine. How much I'm enjoying his company.

I meet lots of attractive, interesting men, but they seem to only want one thing from me.

Royal is in a class of his own.

I've never wanted to touch someone quite this badly.

Just breathing the same air as him feels incredibly intimate.

"Shrimp?" I ask, holding up the one I've just dipped in cocktail sauce.

He opens his mouth and I pop it inside, but before I can pull my hand free, he closes his lips around my fingers, lightly sucking them in.

His eyes don't leave mine.

And all I can do is stare into his handsome face.

He's rugged and chiseled and...powerful. That's the only word that comes to mind. It's not a physical attribute—though he's certainly masculine—so much as an aura. He exudes sex and raw virility, and I can't tear my eyes away as he slowly sucks the remnants of the cocktail sauce off my fingers.

"Delicious," he says in a gruff voice.

I might have licked my lips.

I can't be sure because I'm a little starstruck.

Mesmerized.

Smitten.

Good grief, I'm turning into a teenage girl.

The way he looks at me is so hot I can't seem to help myself.

"M-more?" I whisper in a voice that doesn't sound like my own.

"Absolutely." His blue eyes turn a shade of navy I've never seen before and I can barely remember where the dish of shrimp is.

Because I'm desperate for more contact.

And he doesn't disappoint.

This time, his lips are firmer, sucking harder, and I'm captivated.

What would it feel like if that was my—

I squirm just thinking about it.

"My turn," he says, reaching for a piece of shrimp and dipping it in the cocktail sauce.

My mouth opens before I can think about what I'm doing, and I close my lips around his fingers.

This is ridiculously erotic.

Have I ever sucked a man's fingers before?

It doesn't matter because nothing could be sexier than this.

This moment.

This man.

"You're so fucking beautiful," he murmurs, pulling his fingers away.

I can't seem to think of a response, so I reach out and put my hand on the side of his face, gently rubbing my thumb along the chiseled jaw and cheekbones.

"I'm really glad you came tonight," I say quietly.

"Me too."

"I love your voice…"

He almost smiles.

Almost.

CHAPTER FIVE

Royal

I CAN'T REMEMBER the last time I spent so long talking to a woman.

Hell, I can't remember the last time I spent so long talking to *anyone*.

But there's something about Jade that…

Well, I can't keep my distance.

Normally, it's so easy to throw up barriers, to keep a careful space between myself and the rest of the world.

Jade is—

I want to do a fuck-ton more than just suck at her fingers.

I settle my hand on her lower back as we descend the stairs in Rico's front yard and make our way to her car. She shivers and I shrug out of my jacket, settling it over her shoulders, giving in to the urge to wrap my arm around her waist and draw her close.

Another shiver has me bringing her even closer.

"Better?" I ask.

A nod. "Yes," she says, her voice threaded with heat that wraps its fingers around my dick and squeezes. "Thanks."

"Any time."

As in, I'll touch her any fucking time she'll let me.

Her driver tugs open the door, holding it as we get in.

"Thanks," Jade murmurs, sliding across the seat to give me space to get in.

The door closes with a soft thunk but I'm barely paying attention—because all of that sliding has caused the hem of her skirt to drag up…

Miles and miles of bare skin.

Strong calves, thighs I want to clasp…right before I spread them and feast on the beauty between her legs. The hint of an ass that deserves to be worshipped—

"Royal?"

The soft way she says my name has me jerking my gaze up to her eyes, see the knowing glint in those deep gray depths.

"I'm not going to apologize for getting caught looking at that beautiful body," I murmur, sliding closer, trailing my fingertips up the outside of her thigh, dragging the material higher, until I'm running them lightly along the curve of that lush ass.

"I'm not asking for an apology," she says.

Confident words, but the flush of pink spreads on her cheeks.

Inexperienced, maybe.

Tends to be shy, definitely.

Only…not with me.

My dick goes hard.

"What *are* you asking for?"

That blush grows, but she holds my eyes and I feel myself slipping a little deeper down the treacherous slope of infatuation.

Of obsession.

I felt it once before.

With…Amber.

That name sliding through my mind threatens to douse my erection, to send me right the fuck out of this car. Thankfully, she keeps talking, snapping me out of it.

"A kiss."

My gaze whips back to hers and I lift a brow. "Just one?"

Her lips part, eyes widening, but I don't bother waiting for an answer.

I wrap my fingers around one of her slender wrists and tug, sending her toppling into my lap. She gasps as I drop my mouth to hers, tasting that sound on my tongue.

Tasting her moan as her lips meld to mine, groaning in return as she settles more firmly on top of me, her skirt hiking up, exposing the tops of her thighs, giving me a glimpse of black lace and slick pink and—

Her hand slides into my hair, gripping the strands as she leans closer, deepening the kiss, settling more heavily onto me.

Soft heat.

Fuck, she's sweet.

And sexy as hell as she starts rocking on me, riding the hard ridge of my erection as I take my fill of her mouth. Sleek darts of her tongue, plump lips, moans vibrating through her chest, which is pressed to mine.

Lean curves.

Great tits.

Spectacular ass.

I settle my hands onto the lush curves, draw her flush against me, grinding my hips up into her.

"Oh God!" Her head falls back, her pelvis rocking against mine. "I— That's good," she whispers, her hand in my hair tightening as she moves faster. "*Royal.*"

I slide my hands forward, dip my thumbs under the hem of her underwear.

Smooth, bare skin.

Plump lips.

Slick, *slick* heat.

Whir!

I still, glance over her shoulder and see that the window separating us from the driver has slid down a couple of inches.

"Ms. Cantrell?" the driver calls and I'm pleased to see that he doesn't lower the window any further.

Discreet.

I like it.

Jade may not fully trust her team, but her driver may be a person to keep.

"Yes, John?" she asks, voice remarkably steady despite the desire glazing those storm cloud gray eyes.

"Would you like me to drop you or Mr. Ewing off first?"

My heart skips a beat.

I don't want to go home to my empty house, don't want to leave.

Not just yet.

Our eyes connect and I see the question in her eyes. "Do you want—?"

"Yes."

Gray eyes warming, the storm clouds fading into a foggy morning, perfect for staying in bed and fucking the day away. Her fingers tighten slightly in my hair and then she exhales. "John?"

"Yes, ma'am?"

"You can drop us both at my hotel."

My dick twitches, and I slide my thumbs in a little further, grazing the sensitive skin at the apex of her thighs, loving the way she moans softly, her head falling back, her hips jerking forward. "Royal," she whispers, instinctually shifting closer, seeking out my fingers.

"That's it, baby," I murmur, "let me in."

Her legs widen.

I slip in a little closer, parting her slick folds, tracing a fingertip along the seam of her.

She gasps quietly.

"You've got it, ma'am," John says and I barely hear the glass separating us whirring back up.

Because I'm too focused on Jade.

On the way my name tumbles off her lips. On the way she instinctively seeks out the purchase of my hand. On her silky skin and soaked pussy and her breasts pressing against the fabric of the short, tight dress she changed into earlier.

I circle her entrance, push inside, feel her immediately clamp down around my finger.

Fuck, I want that pussy tightening around my cock.

Patience.

"I—" She reaches for me. "You—"

"Shh, baby," I order quietly. "Let me make you feel good."

She melts around me—inside and out, moisture gathering, soaking my fingers and palm, her body softening, slumping against me.

Trusting me.

Even though I'm broken and grumpy and an asshole to almost everyone in the world.

Not to the people I care about.

And inexplicably…not to Jade.

There's a niggling in the back of my head, but one I can't allow myself to consider, not right now. Too dangerous. Too fucking stupid.

I just want to enjoy this moment.

Enjoy this slick cunt and sweet woman who I intend on reducing to a limp puddle of goo.

And with that thought, I focus, sliding my finger in deep, curling it up to tease the sensitive nerves on the inside of her pussy. She gasps, hands clamping onto my arms, nails biting into my skin, hips jerking.

There then.

She likes it right fucking *there.*

Grinning, I begin working her in earnest, drawing my finger out, sliding it back in, stroking until her breath begins to catch, until she's soft enough for me to slip another finger in, until her hips begin moving in rapid pumps, until her pussy flutters around me, until—

"Royal!"

She comes apart *on* me.

"Oh God," she whispers. "Oh my fracking God."

I still, wondering if I heard her right, but then I realize that we've pulled to a stop, realize that she looks like I've just spent the last twenty minutes making out and finger-fucking her, realize that I have the fucking boner to end all boners, realize—

That I need to stop thinking about making her come again (even if it's definitely going to happen again and in short order).

Cursing softly, I gently slip my fingers from her, lips tipping up at the shocked expression on her face as I lift them to my mouth and suck.

"Sweet," I murmur, reaching down and straightening her underwear, tugging the hem of her dress down. "I knew you'd taste sweet."

She shivers and I tuck my coat around her again, covering that tempting body.

Then I snag her purse and position it strategically (the boner to end all boners shows no sign of dissipating) as the back door opens a crack and John asks, "Ready?"

Yeah, he knew exactly what we've been up to back here.

And he knows how to be discreet.

Definitely a keeper.

I give Jade another once over, see that all the pertinent bits are covered then call out, "Yup."

The door swings wide and I step out, blocking the view of her exit from any asshole who might be around to snap a picture of her in a compromising position. As I do so, I notice that John has brought us to the hotel's back entrance.

Yup. The man needs a raise.

I make a mental note to mention that to her.

Later.

Much later.

Because now I'm focused on escorting her into the hotel… and up to her room.

I slip John a hundred, then give another to the staff member holding the back door open, and we get into the freight elevator, hit the button for her floor.

She's leaning heavily against me, her lips swollen and those cheeks still flushed, her body trembling as we ascend. Both of us are silent as we listen to the elevator move, as we wait for the doors to open.

Finally, after what seems like a fucking eternity, they slide open with a soft screech.

We step off and head down the hall.

"I need—"

I dig out the keycard from her purse, pass it over.

She takes it, swipes it over the keypad, and I push the heavy panel inward, holding it for her to walk in before me, my eyes drifting to those miles and miles of bare skin, the hem of her dress and my jacket flirting with her the underside of her ass.

I need them off her.

I need *her.*

I allow the door to swing shut, flick the deadbolt, and turn back to her…

"Get naked."

CHAPTER SIX

Jade

THE TIMBRE of his voice as he tells me to "Get naked" makes my insides flood with desire.

The memory of what we did in the car sends me right back into a state of arousal, and that says something because my sexual appetite is pretty small. Almost non-existent. I enjoy an orgasm as much as anyone, but I prefer them to be self-induced. The fact that Royal could do what he did, and elicit that much of a reaction from me, is pretty freakin' amazing.

And I want more.

So I let my dress fall to the floor and step out of it.

That leaves me in nothing but my super push-up bra and matching lace thong panties.

"Fuck. Me. You're breathtaking."

His voice is low, growly, and probably the sexiest sound I've ever heard.

"Now put your hands on the wall and show me what a good girl you are."

I comply like someone else is controlling me—*why am I putting my hands on the wall?!*—because I move quickly.

Seriously, why does my vagina love that demanding tone so much?

"Oh, this is nice," I murmur as I feel him behind me even though he hasn't touched me yet.

Heat. A tiny rush of air as he moves. The rustle of clothing.

A slight tickle from his hair as he leans close.

"It's going to turn not-so-nice in a minute—are you ready for me, baby?"

All I can do is nod because I'm incapable of sound at the moment.

He drops to his knees—at least I think so—because he's nuzzling the small of my back. The scruff of his beard is rough against my skin but I like it. It's part of him, his touch, the way he makes me feel, and my body is in a heightened state of awareness.

I start to reach back, to touch him, to feel him, to discern the way he's touching me, but he stops me.

"Hands. On. The. *Wall.*"

I'm not religious but the barked order makes me a believer of something. Maybe the cult of Royal.

Because I'll do anything he asks.

"Don't move."

Like I even could.

He runs a hand along my side, pausing to cup and squeeze one ass cheek as he presses light kisses along the bumps of my spine.

"So fucking perfect," he murmurs, letting his mouth travel lower.

He kisses my hip, the outside of my thigh, and then takes a gentle bite of my ass. No one's ever done anything like this before, and the sensations feel so good that I'm rooted in place. A whimper escapes me as he pulls away and I both feel and hear the vibration of his chuckle.

"Don't worry, baby, I'm not going anywhere." A beat, his hand trailing lower. "As long as you don't move."

One edge of my underwear slides down, then the other, and it takes all of my self-control not to wiggle. Not to jut out my backside to get more friction, more of a connection.

I want him so much I can barely breathe.

But I'm also not naive.

"You have a condom?" I ask in a rush. "If not—"

"Of course." The bossy growl is gone and my heart squeezes as I realize he's letting me know I'm safe. "I would never do anything to hurt you. Physically or otherwise."

I somehow already knew that—because he wouldn't be here if I didn't—but it's nice to hear the words.

And it makes me want him that much more.

He presses something cool and scratchy against my side and I glance down, spying the familiar square packet. "Condom. Right here for when we need it. Okay?"

"Yes. Thank you."

"Now spread your legs, baby."

I move my feet apart and he nudges at the inside of my thigh. "More."

How is it that I'm equal parts aroused and embarrassed? He's staring at the crack of my ass and my vagina. His mouth—*oh sweet Jesus*—is in the most amazing place, doing something that can only be described as magical. It only takes a few flicks of his tongue before it takes too much effort to hold up my head and my forehead hits the wall.

"Royal..." His name is a whisper on my lips but he hears me. Fingers dig into my hip, holding me firmly in place as he continues sliding his tongue up toward a place no one has ever touched like this. I want to fidget, say something to stop him, but I can't.

I don't really want to. Whatever he wants to do, I'm going to let him.

I don't know why.

All I know is how good it feels.

Using his mouth and hand, he's got me spread open, and I feel like a veritable feast.

It's both wicked and deeply satisfying in a way I've never experienced before.

When he slides his tongue inside of me, a moan escapes that I can't hold back. He follows with a finger and it's even better in this position than when we'd been in the limo. My feet move even wider apart, giving him better access, and he adds a second finger, scissoring them lightly.

"Oh please…" I groan impatiently. "Please, Royal…"

"This is just a warm-up, beautiful."

He pulls out his fingers and slowly stands up, his body moving along mine. I want to protest, but he doesn't give me time to.

"Open your mouth."

When I do, he slips in the fingers he'd just pulled out of me.

"Lick them clean."

I close my lips around them and do exactly as he commands.

"So pretty when you suck like that…it would be even prettier if that was my cock, but right now, I have something else in mind." I hear the rustle of clothing, feel him step out of his pants. The crinkle of plastic as he tears open the condom.

Holy guacamole, this is really happening.

Then he's between my legs, thick and hard against my entrance, pushing inside.

He's bigger than I'm used to, but I love how it feels as he spreads me open. Just when I think he has to be all the way in, he pushes in another inch, and it's excruciatingly erotic.

"I knew you'd be a good girl," he murmurs, pressing his body tight against mine. "You like my cock inside of you?"

"Yes…so much."

I feel a hand at the middle of my back and realize that my bra is still on.

Well, it *was*.

Because he's just flung it across the room.

He pulls out to the tip and then thrusts up deep.

"Oh, God." I whimper because it's taking some adjustment to stretch out enough to accommodate his girth. And length.

Jesus, he's huge.

"Relax," he whispers, pressing soft kisses on the side of my neck. "Just keep your hands on the wall and let me show you how good it can be. I promise, you'll be begging me for more before this is over."

I moan at the contrasting sensations of being practically impaled on his dick while the flutter of his lips on the skin of my neck is the tenderest of caresses.

He glides in and out slowly now, and I feel every inch pulsing through me.

It's still a little uncomfortable, but pleasure is rapidly overtaking everything else.

"Royal, I need—"

"All you need to do is stand there and take it," he rumbles.

He uses his teeth to graze the skin of my shoulder, and I shudder at how much I like the roughness. It's new to me, but my knees wobble with the ferocity of what's happening to my body. I want to move but it's truly impossible in this position, and he's driving into me now with deep, measured thrusts that steal my breath each time he bottoms out.

"Royal, please!"

"Told you you'd beg." He picks up speed and my vagina clenches in anticipation of what's coming.

"That's it—squeeze my cock with that pretty pink cunt."

My head falls back. "Oh, God."

I'm going to come again.

I'm so full, stretched to what has to be my limit, yet it's intoxicating. I need more. *Everything*. For him to make it hurt so good.

And he does.

"Royal!"

He thrusts into me with so much force my feet leave the ground and I am literally impaled on him.

But it doesn't matter.

Nothing does.

My body is spinning out of control, my climax building from deep in my belly. I feel it coiling, tightening, sending pinpricks of pleasure throughout my vagina.

"Come for me, beautiful girl," he growls. "Let me feel you take everything I've got."

Yeah, that's it for me.

I sputter out something nonsensical, and then I crash over the edge with a scream. I've never made a sound like that before, but I can't help myself. I've lost all sense of control, reason, and thought—all I can do is take what he's offered.

"*Fuck!*" His grunt of pleasure is followed by a wild jerking motion, and I feel him throbbing inside of me.

"Don't stop," I plead.

And he doesn't.

Thrusting and pulsing until we're both spent.

Spineless masses that can't move.

Thank goodness my hands are still braced on the wall because I'm not sure I could stay upright if they weren't.

"Damn, baby, that was beautiful." His voice is raw, filled with an emotion I can't quite decipher.

"Holy guacamole," I blearily croak. "What did you just do to us?"

"Holy guacamole?" He chuckles, presses a kiss to the top of my head, and I can practically hear the sexy smile in his next words. "Fucking adorable. And if you don't know what we just did, baby, we're going to have to make sure you *fully* understand."

My brows pull together. "How?"

"By doing it again."

Suddenly, I'm completely lucid.

And even wetter.

"Yes, please."

Without warning, he pulls out and wraps an arm around my

waist. He lifts me like I weigh nothing, tossing me over his left shoulder, his arm firm around my thighs.

He dumps me on the bed and follows, moving his larger body over mine, his mouth immediately seeking my lips.

And we're off and running again.

I should be sated, but I'm not.

I want more.

Everything.

Again.

Repeatedly.

"Royal…"

"I'm right here, baby," he murmurs against my skin. "Not going anywhere."

But that's a lie.

Because when I wake up in the morning, the space beside me is cold and the room chillingly empty.

Like he was never here.

CHAPTER SEVEN

Royal

"LOOK, UNCLE ROYAL!"

Frankie, my niece in everything but blood, runs toward me, her dark brown hair flying behind, little backpack hanging on her shoulders. She's clutching a paper in her hand, one she shoves in my face the moment I bend down and scoop her up.

I wave at her teacher, then the receptionist, and push through the preschool's door, stepping back out into the sunny SoCal winter day.

The only thing that makes it winter is that it's a brisk fifty degrees instead of summer's nineties or hundreds.

My lips twitch.

God, my blood's gotten thin if fifty degrees is *brisk*.

"Look, Uncle Royal," Frankie says again, holding up the paper a second time. "Look what I made!"

I lean back enough to get a glimpse of the collection of stick figures and smile. "Is that you and your mom?"

"Yup," she says with a pop of the P. "And there's you and Uncle Atlas and Uncle Dash and Uncle Banks." She points to each of the squiggles. "And there's Auntie Aspen."

"What's that?" I ask as I open the car door and set her into her seat, supervising her as she buckles in.

She's a big girl and likes to do *all* the things herself.

So, I've learned to give in on this one—and by give in, I mean I let her put the snaps in and then distract her so I can adjust the buckles to make sure she's safe.

"That's the baby in Auntie Aspen's belly."

"Oh, that's nice." I grab the strap and pull, straightening the buckle and securing my little princess. "Do you think it's going to be a boy or a girl?" I ask, knowing it'll be a bit before they have the scan to find out for sure.

"A girl!" she says, arms shooting up, nearly giving me a papercut to my eye in the process.

"Because you want another girl to play with or because you really think that?"

Her face screws up as she considers my question, and I press a kiss to the top of her head, bend out of the car and climb into the driver's seat. I buckle in, hating the dulled sensation in my right hand. I'm lucky, I guess—even though it sure as fuck doesn't feel like that—but logically I know I am.

I struggle with the fine motor shit—like hitting the right chords on my guitar—but at least I can do this: pick up the little girl who's still considering my question in the back seat, get this time with her, and help Briar out when she deserves a fucking medal for being there for me these last couple of years.

Yes, that's what family does.

Or at least what *this* family we've built does.

Her life was upended by the pregnancy, by the deadbeat asshole who skipped out on her.

We were there for her—me, Banks, Atlas, and Dash, of course, and hers and Dash's parents are great. But she went from a college student to a mom.

And she was chronically independent (still is), didn't want to ask for help unless she was desperate (still doesn't), worked—*works*—hard to provide for herself, even though we would have all chipped in financially to take care of both of them (and still would).

It's better now, but it got so bad there for a while that we had to almost bully her into accepting our help.

Thankfully, we got through the stubbornness, she moved out to California, and things have been better since.

We all have a solid family unit.

She gets regular breaks.

And I get to have my Frankie time.

"I *think* it's going to be a girl," she says, finally done pondering my question. "Plus, Mom says that we do *not* need another man in our family."

I chuckle. "Why's that?"

"She said…"

My gaze flicks to the rearview, and I see the scrunched up look of concentration. I give her time to remember, to find the words. She's extremely verbal for her age, but sometimes she gets frustrated when she can't get out the words she has in her head.

So, I give her that time as I back out of the stall and carefully navigate my way through the school's parking lot—because tiny humans.

"She said it's because of test tone!"

I pull to a stop at the signal, taking a moment to ferret that one out.

It's Briar, so really, it could be anything—there's a reason her nickname is Thorny.

But this…takes that moment.

"Testosterone?" I ask when the pieces eventually come together.

"Yup." Another pop on her P, her legs swinging (and thus, kicking the back of my seat in a regular interval). "You guys have too much of it."

I grin but change the subject before I say something that will no doubt get back to Briar and get me in trouble. "So who'd you play with at school today?"

"Felix and I did blocks. And then Ms. Mya pushed me on the swings before we did our letter of the day. Did you know that giraffe starts with G?"

"It does?" I tease.

A beleaguered sigh that's far too old for her years. "Uncle *Royal*."

I grin. "You know what else starts with G?"

"What?"

"Goose."

A pause as she decides if that passes muster. "What else?"

"Why don't you tell *me?*"

Another sigh. "Why don't we take turns?"

Negotiating. She's definitely Briar's daughter through and through. There's a reason Ms. Thorny has become Atlas's right hand woman.

She's smart as hell, ruthless when she has to be, and she's a master negotiator.

"Works for me. But you're next."

I flick my gaze to the mirror again before concentrating on the road again, but the glimpse of her face scrunched with concentration makes me smile.

It's easy to be with her.

Easy to think about nothing except for silly conversations and words that start with the letter G and how tall the tower of blocks she built was and what snack she had after lunch.

It's much easier to focus on Frankie than think about…

A tiny blond bombshell.

A dress crumpled on the floor.

A sleeping goddess left naked in a hotel bed.

"Goat!"

I brutally shove the image of Jade from my head, something I've had to do far too many times over the past two weeks.

I know it was a dick move to leave like that.

But…

I'd wanted to stay.

So, I *had* to go.

"What's yours, Uncle Royal?"

Christ.

I slam the lid on all thoughts of Jade Cantrell. "Gemstone."

"Gas."

"Gas *can*," I say on my turn.

"Uncle *Royal*," she says, her disapproval clear.

"Game," I provide instead.

"Good."

I turn onto her street. "Is that your answer or are you telling me I did a good job?"

She giggles. "Both."

"Oh." I pause. "Okay."

"What's *your* next one?"

"Gorilla," I say as I pull into the driveway and shove the gearshift into park.

"Hey, that's what *I* was going to say!"

"Hmm." I snag her backpack from the floor, her picture from when I'd set it on the passenger's seat, get out of my SUV, and help her down from the back (she's even better at unbuckling than she is buckling). "Well, I guess you'll have to think of another one."

Scowling, she grabs her picture as we make our way up to the front door.

I let us in.

"Grass!"

"That's a good one."

She smiles proudly. "And I have another."

"What's that?"

"Guitar!"

The feelings sweep over me in a way I both love and hate—because I used to love playing the guitar and nowadays I love teaching Frankie how to play, and because I hate that I can't do what I used to, and…

I hate that it makes me think of a certain collection of chords on a certain song that just won a certain blond bombshell a very important award.

And, of course, while I'm feeling all of that, processing it all, trying to shove it all down so I don't have to think about it—

Briar walks into the room.

She's on a call, but she still clocks whatever is on my face because she hangs up almost immediately.

And though she greets Frankie and oohs and aahs over the drawing and asks all the right questions about her daughter's day at school, her focus hasn't completely left me.

Case in point?

How she reacts when I sidle to the door.

"Why don't you go sit at the table, honey?" she tells Frankie. "I put your snack out."

"'Kay!" Frankie says, running into the other room.

Briar turns to face me but doesn't say anything.

"What?" I ask into the terse quiet that falls.

She just crosses her arms and lifts her brows.

But I've had far too much experience with the glares that Briar can dish out to crack that easily.

"I need to get home."

"Right," she says, telling me she knows exactly what bullshit that is. "Well, you can go…"

I start to turn again.

"Right after you tell me what the fuck is going on."

"I have the pool guy coming. We think there might be a leak in the spa."

"*I* dealt with the pool guy last week."

Fuck.

Her brows flick up again. "Now spill."

"I—" My mind is racing for a believable excuse—the last thing I need is for Briar to get an inkling for exactly how fucked up my head is right now.

Thankfully, the universe is on my side for once.

Because her cell rings.

"I'll let you get that," I say. "Tell Frankie I'll see her Thursday for our guitar lesson."

"Royal—"

Ring-ring.

I kiss her cheek, tug a strand of her hair. "Bye, Thorny." I raise my voice. "Bye, Tater Tot!"

"Bye, Uncle Royal!" I hear, though the words are muffled by that snack she's devouring.

Briar sighs. "Roy—"

Ring-ring.

"Later," I mutter.

And then I get the hell out.

I know I dodged a bullet.

Same as I know I need to get my head together before I see them again.

The last thing I need is for my family to know exactly what I was feeling that night in the hotel room.

And how I'm fucking terrified that it might have changed everything.

CHAPTER EIGHT

Jade

I've been in a funk since the night of the awards ceremony, and no matter how many times I tell myself I'm better off without a broody, grumpy songwriter with the world's biggest penis, it's hard to let go. Of the memories. The laughter. The sex. Good gracious, I've never experienced anything like what we did. What *he* did.

Including the waking up alone part.

In what universe do you do that to someone you spent the whole night with? I've had one-night stands, but those were hookups. Meet, have a drink, have sex, say goodbye. Even with a one-nighter, you say goodbye? Right?

Well, okay. I've had one—two, if you count Royal.

But we said goodbye when it was over. It was polite. Civilized. Frankly, I was glad for him to go because the sex had been unremarkable. With the first guy. Sex with Royal, well, I probably won't get over that for a very long time.

Or him.

I'm not in love or anything stupid, but we connected in a way I've never felt with any other guy. By the time we left Rico's, we were finishing each other's sentences. He likes so many of the same things I do. He understands my life, my career, and what it means to be on top.

And he thinks it's adorable that I don't use curse words.

Thanks, Grandma Louise.

She pounded it into my brain that a lady doesn't use those words. Never, ever. Except maybe during childbirth. She told me that was the only time she ever said shit.

I smile at the memory and dab a bit of gloss onto my lips.

It's time to stop moping about one very annoying Royal-pain-in-the-butt.

That's how I'll think of him from now on.

If I think of him at all.

I grab my purse and head into the hallway, where my security detail is waiting to escort me down to the car that will take me to the interview I'm doing with 'Modern Country Music' magazine.

"Good morning." My publicist, Farrah Henley, is waiting in the car. "Are you ready? They sent over a list of questions but I don't think you need to look at them. Really basic stuff. They want to know how you felt when you won, stuff like that."

"Okay, great." I nod, pulling out my cell phone, and checking my texts. I'd originally planned to head back to Nashville after the awards show, but it's been one thing after another over the last two weeks. Interviews, a morning show appearance, and now they want me to sing the national anthem at the SoCal Vipers' game tomorrow night. *Then* I can go home.

Home.

The word has a strange connotation these days.

Is it a home now that it's so empty?

Mom and Grandma Louise are both gone. Mom died when I was in middle school and Grandma Louise just eighteen months ago.

And now I'm alone.

I have cousins and friends, a handful of staff that run the

farm, and of course, my career, but it *feels* like I'm alone. Except for those stolen hours with Royal-pain-in-the-butt.

Nope. Not going there. Not today.

We arrive at the meeting place—a tall building with glass windows that goes up higher than I can see from this angle. I like how majestic it is. It somehow makes me feel safe, like I can hide within it and never see anyone unless I want to. Maybe I'll sell my farm and buy a condo in a really tall building like this.

Yeah, right.

I do a mental head shake and step out of the limo.

"Good morning! I'm Becky. I'll be escorting you up to see Ms. Bancroft."

"Thank you," I murmur politely.

"Is there sparkling water?" Farrah asks her. "I'm parched. It's on Ms. Cantrell's list."

"Of course." Becky nods, chattering with Farrah as we get on the elevator.

I tune them out because I'm mentally drained. It's been a long couple of weeks. My phone has been ringing nonstop since the award show. Invitations, questions, requests…people always want something from me. I began to notice it in the last year, but it's ramped up to a thousand since I won Song of the Year. I really hate saying no, but I'm already spread a little thin. It's hard to be in twenty places at once, *and* work on my music, *and* think about the next album, *and* play gigs.

"Jade. Hello. I'm Liza Bancroft."

"Nice to meet you, Liza." I smile at the journalist because she looks a lot like my mama, with big blond hair and a little too much blue eyeshadow. I'm momentarily lost in a memory of my mom teaching me how to do my makeup, not long before the cancer made it so she couldn't do much of anything, and it's times like this I miss her so much it's hard to breathe.

"If it's okay with you," Liza says, "we can settle in and have a casual conversation. Like two girlfriends."

I'm immediately on alert, all warm fuzzies gone, replaced

with wariness. Whenever a journalist says something like that, it means she's going to get serious with the questions even though Farrah said they were all pretty basic.

"I do *love* having girlfriends," I say, in my heaviest southern drawl. People automatically equate that accent with both stupidity and naivete; she's about to find out otherwise.

She fidgets for a moment and then takes out her phone, pushing some buttons. She's recording us, obviously, and I'm starting to feel uneasy. I've always been something of an empath, and I can usually tell what someone is thinking.

Except Royal-pain-in-the-butt.

He blindsided me by leaving.

Knock it off, I chide myself. *Stop thinking about him.*

"So you're coming off an amazing win for Song of the Year," Liza says, jumping right in. "How did that feel?"

"Amazing," I reply. "I honestly wasn't expecting it. When they said my name, it took a second to register."

"You looked beautiful," she says. "And your speech was touching. You didn't seem nervous at all."

"Thank you."

"Did you know Royal Ewing would be there?"

My internal bullcrap detector immediately goes off.

"No." I slowly shake my head. "We'd never met or had any type of contact."

"But you left together."

Good grief.

Where is she going with this?

I glance at Farrah, but she's busy on her phone, completely ignoring the conversation.

"We met backstage and wound up going to a party at Rico Galago's house."

"Was it a date?" She smiles, a teasing tone to her voice, but now I know where she's going and I refuse to play this kind of game.

"Of course not. I told you—we just met. We wanted to talk a

little since he wrote the song for me. So, we decided to go to the party."

"He was seen leaving your hotel room early the next morning."

I freeze.

My cheeks feel warm, and my stomach feels like it's going to turn.

What the heck is going on?

I look to Farrah but she's not even paying attention, tapping away on her phone without a care in the world.

"Is there a question?" I ask quietly, grateful my hands are on my lap so I can squeeze my thighs to vent my frustration without anyone seeing me.

"What were you two doing all night?"

I snort. "We were doing what musicians do—talking about and writing music."

"Is he writing you a new song?"

"You'll just have to wait and see with everyone else." I try to keep my voice playful, but I'm furious on the inside.

I don't like getting blindsided like this. The record company's PR people usually protect me from questions like this, but of course, I've also never had anyone spotted leaving my hotel room before either.

My management team hired Farrah when 'Forever in Rewind' started to take off, insisting that we needed someone who would have the time to focus on just me, instead of an entire record label's roster of talent. I don't think she's particularly good at her job, but she does what needs to be done.

Until today.

And we're going to have a conversation about it ASAP.

Despite my annoyance with him, Royal's words about having the right people in your corner have been percolating in the back of my mind, and I realize I'm not truly surrounded by a team of trustworthy people.

I'm going to have to do something about that.

Thankfully, the rest of the interview is pretty bland—despite multiple references to Royal—but I'm still furious when we get back out to the limo. The moment we pull into traffic I turn to Farrah, who's immersed in something on her phone.

"Farrah." I say her name, and she doesn't even look up.

"Give me a minute," she mutters.

I wait ten seconds, counting slowly.

...one thousand and nine, one thousand and ten...

"Time's up," I say, a little louder this time.

She glances up with an arched brow. "What's wrong?"

"Why didn't you or your team know that Royal was spotted leaving my hotel room?"

She looks confused for a second but then shrugs. "I'm sure someone did, but it's not a huge deal."

"It is to me."

"Why?" She shrugs. "He's hot. Every woman in America wishes he could be seen leaving their room."

"That's a fantasy," I grit out. "This is my real life."

"It's not a big deal, Jade. Seriously, don't get your panties in a bunch." She goes back to her phone.

"Farrah!" I raise my voice this time, and she puts her phone down with a put-upon sigh.

"What would you like me to do?" she asks. "It's already over."

"You needed to step in when Liza brought that up. You said the questions they sent were basic. And they weren't. She brought up Royal at every opportunity, and I had to deflect. It's supposed to be your job to make sure that doesn't happen."

"You handled her great!" she says, with a placating smile. "The interview is going to be amazing and—"

"You're missing the point."

"Look, I know this level of fame is new to you, but you're good at this stuff. And mentioning Royal isn't a bad thing. Any chance we get to capitalize on your friendship with him is a huge bonus."

I want to snap that we're not friends, but that's more information than she needs.

Especially since I've just made a decision about what I'm going to do.

"I don't need to capitalize on any of my *friendships,*" I say quietly. "My music speaks for itself. As my publicist, you should know that."

"Well, yeah, but your connection to Royal is different. He's an enigma and never more so than since his accident. The music rumor mill is still buzzing about the way his wife divorced him afterward and how he and his band aren't speaking. It's enthralling."

"It's terrible," I snap, irritated. "He lost his ability to play guitar, which was his career. On top of that, his wife and band all abandoned him…What part of that is enthralling? Anyone with a soul should feel awful. And as a human being, the story is heartbreaking."

She rolls her eyes. "Yeah, I'm sure he's breaking hearts all the way to the bank. Every time a story goes viral, they sell a ton of records, and no matter what happens going forward, he makes money from that. We should all be so lucky to be in his situation."

Is she serious right now?

I never liked her, but now…I truly hate her.

Will I go to jail if I reach out and slap both sides of her face a few times?

Probably.

Not worth it.

But I feel better knowing what I'm about to do.

"I don't think this is working," I say quietly.

"What isn't?" she asks, frowning.

"This. You. Me. Working together."

"What does that mean?"

"You're fired."

CHAPTER NINE

Royal

"Is Uncle Banks going to get lots of goals tonight?" Frankie asks as she skips her way across the concourse, knowing the way to the box that Atlas reserves for Vipers home games like the little princess she is.

Perks of having an uncle on the roster.

Perks of having a billionaire for another uncle.

What perks do I afford her?

Chauffeur services and guitar lessons.

I do my best to remain inconspicuous as we weave through the crowd. We're not far from L.A., so seeing a celebrity walking around isn't all that unusual, and I've been to enough of Banks's games over the years that the regulars don't get all bent out of shape.

But ever since the awards show—

No, ever since Jade announced that we were working on new music…

I've been getting more attention than usual.

Attention. Fuck. I used to crave it, used to live for it, used to think it could sustain me when nothing else could.

But now I hate it.

I can feel all the stares closing in on me, making my nape itch and my lungs tighten. It's hard to draw in a full breath, hard to think clearly like I have to with Frankie at my side.

Briar's trusting me to look after her, to make sure she's safe.

And yeah, I have security. And yeah, they're currently flanking us as we make our way to the suite, but this is Frankie.

She's all of our hearts.

So, I pull my head out of my ass and focus.

"I'm sure Uncle Banks will do his best to score tonight."

"More goals are better."

My lips turn up at the edges. "I think Uncle Banks would agree with you."

"Can I get popcorn?"

I flick my gaze at my security, and he nods, pivoting us to the concession stand. I could probably send him out to get some after we get settled in the suite.

But we're already watching the game from a suite.

And Frankie already has a rock star, a hockey player, and a billionaire for uncles.

Waiting in line for her popcorn is good for her.

So, we do that—and end up with candy and sodas and nachos for our trouble. And by the time we've pushed into the suite and taken our seats, the main lights are dimming over the arena and the announcer's voice is booming over the speakers.

"Put your hands together for tonight's performer of the national anthem—none other than Song of the Year winner, Jade Cantrell."

My pulse is thundering through my veins, echoing through my eardrums louder than the crowd's cheers—and they're pretty fucking loud, the applause radiating through the arena as Jade walks down the red carpet that's been rolled out to center ice.

She's wearing skintight jeans, thigh high boots, and a SoCal Vipers jersey that I want to rip off her.

Hell, I want to rip every bit of clothing off her, and not just because the jersey she's wearing has Banks's fucking last name emblazoned across the shoulder blades.

"Uncle Royal!" Frankie says, jumping up and down, scattering popcorn this way and that.

Aspen is going to kill me when she sees this mess.

But Frankie is far too excited at the prospect of watching Jade Cantrell to realize she's wasting her treat.

I snag it out of her hands and set it, along with the rest of the snacks, on one of the high top tables.

"Is she gonna sing, Uncle Royal? Is she?"

I nod, and even though my voice is steady when I say, "Yes," my heart is anything but.

Even the way she walks that carpet to pause in the spotlight is something special.

And when she opens her mouth and starts belting out the words to 'The Star Spangled Banner,' I'm captivated.

Lost in the effortless way her voice carries through the arena, completely taken by the minuscule movements in her expression, the emotion in her frame.

She feels every word.

And she's fucking incredible.

Just like she was in that hotel room, her cheeks flushed, her lips swollen, her tight cunt clamping around my cock as we came together again and again and *again.*

I'm supposed to forget that night.

Move on.

Go back to normal.

But…I can't fucking tear my eyes away from her.

I hardly realize that the song's over, and it's only the lights coming on and her disappearing into the depths of the arena that bring me back into myself.

Frankie is vibrating with excitement, dancing around like a kid who's never going to sleep tonight (even though I'm almost positive that she'll crash the moment we hit the highway, like she always does), and that excitement ramps up when the guys take their positions and line up for the start of the game.

There's a whistle and ref releases the puck, and then my niece is hyper-focused on the action below.

Banks corralling the puck and skating with it on his stick, deking around some traffic to move hard into the zone. The Sierra are on him, though, the contact hard enough to make me wince.

I remember those days, the body-on-body collisions stealing my breath and making my head ring.

I loved playing hockey, was lucky enough to continue that through college.

But I wasn't a lifer.

I wasn't good enough, for one thing.

I didn't have the drive, like Banks does, for another.

My life was my guitar, my band, the rush of a new melody, the roar of the crowd when I hit the solo just right.

The play quickly turns and suddenly, the Vipers are on defense, Banks and company skating hard back to their zone, doing their best to contain the offensive prowess of the Sierra's top line.

Fucking Lake Jordan, man.

I'm so glad I don't have to play against him out there.

He skates the puck in, but Banks gets a good stick on him, knocking the puck away, giving the Vipers' goalie the opportunity to corral it for a whistle and stoppage in play.

As the two teams skate off the ice, swapping lines and players, I'm distracted by movement to my right.

And so is Frankie.

I realize why a second later, my heart threatening to crawl up the back of my throat.

The suite next to us had been empty.

And now—

"It's Jade!" Frankie exclaims, her hand grabbing my bad one. It's instinct to slip it free, to wrap my other hand around hers as she jumps up and down. "Uncle Royal, Jade is next to us! Can we say hi, can we, can we, can we?"

My lungs are going tight.

My pulse is pounding.

The promise of seeing her, talking to her, *touching* her—

I want it so badly that I know I can't fucking allow this to happen.

"Ah, Tater Tot," I begin. "I'm sure Jade just wants to relax with her friends and have a quiet night."

Frankie's face kills me.

The disappointment.

Christ, I can't stand it.

"But she's all alone," Frankie says. "She doesn't have any friends with her, just some men in suits."

The way my niece says that last part sends a blip of guilt through me.

Because she's parroting something she's heard me say far too often.

But I don't comment on it…because my gaze is sliding to the side, seeing Jade at the front of the suite next to us.

And she *is* surrounded by a bunch of fucking guys in suits.

Fuck.

"And don't you know her?" she asks. "You guys made that song together. I'm sure she likes you and wants to talk and stuff."

That almost makes me smile.

Frankie is cute as shit.

But she's also not getting me anywhere near that fucking suite.

That night is far too fresh. The pictures in the media far too prevalent. The fucking interview with the celebrity magazine published far too recently.

This is bad for me.

For my plans to stay out of the limelight and far away from all of the Hollywood bullshit.

For my plans to stay far away from anyone who might hurt me.

"We played on the same song, Tater Tot. But we don't know each other. Not really."

Except I know every inch of her body, have traced my tongue over each and every freckle, tasted her, touched her, felt her body clench around me as she came apart.

"But look, Uncle Royal."

She points, and I can't keep my eyes from Jade's box.

"She looks sad."

Fucking hell, Jade *does* look sad.

Which is why Frankie's next words push me into doing something really fucking stupid.

"Can't we go and cheer her up? Just for a little while?"

CHAPTER TEN

Jade

"Ms. Cantrell?" One of my security guys gently touches my shoulder. "You received a note from someone in one of the other suites."

I sigh.

It's probably an invitation from some corporate CEO who noticed I'm here alone.

The invite could be genuine or an attempt to get their name in the news because Jade Cantrell joined them in their box.

Whoever it is, they're probably watching, so I keep a pleasant smile on my face as I unfold the piece of paper.

And freeze.

Jade—

My goddaughter is a huge fan and wants to meet you. If you could do this for her, I'd appreciate it. We'll keep the visit short.

Royal

Royal.

It's been two weeks and my body still tingles in all the places he touched me.

Which is pretty much everywhere.

Crud.

And I'm sitting here out in the open where he—and anyone else who's noticed me—is watching my reaction.

That's just great.

I honestly never want to see him again, but the goddaughter he told me about is only three. I can and should do this. It's not her fault her godfather is a womanizing cretin.

I nod to my security guy, Larry, and get to my feet as he walks over to open the door.

And there he is…

Royal-pain-in-the-butt.

Looking better than he should, with his scruffy beard and unkempt long hair.

Hair I vividly remember tugging on as he made me—

"Jade!" Frankie's squeal is delightful. Her eyes dance with mischievous excitement as she pulls Royal forward. "Hi!"

"Hi there." I make sure not to have eye contact with Royal as I squat down to my haunches so it's easier to talk to Frankie. "You must be Frankie."

"You know my name?" Her eyes round.

"Royal told me all about you," I respond.

"Uncle Royal told you about me?" She clasps her hands together in front of her chest and grins. "It's cause he loves me."

"I'm sure he does."

"I love love *love* 'Temporary Love Song' and 'Forever in Rewind.' They're my favorites."

"Thank you. 'Temporary Love Song' is the very first song I ever wrote," I tell her. And the only one my record company would let me record. After that, they made me buy them from big-name songwriters. Like Royal Ewing.

I won't tell her that part.

"I want to write songs too," Frankie says. "Uncle Royal is teaching me to play guitar and piano. Then I want to write lots of songs. Better than 'Old MacDonald.' That's so boring." She rolls her eyes dramatically, making me bite back a laugh.

"Well, you have to work your way up," I say.

The crowd goes wild—apparently the Vipers scored—and Frankie's eyes fly to the TV screen on the wall.

"Did Uncle Banks score?" she demands, turning to her uncle.

"No, it was Magnus Forsberg," he replies. "But Uncle Banks got the assist."

"Goals are better," Frankie mumbles, turning back to me.

"They are, but this is a team sport, right? So it takes the whole team to win." I try to be gentle so she doesn't think I'm upset with her.

She knits her little brows together as if considering this carefully. "I guess so. I just like it better when Uncle Banks scores. Did you know my auntie Aspen is going to have a baby?"

I chuckle at the sharp right in conversation. "No, I didn't."

She gives me the rundown on what everyone in her inner circle is doing—Uncle Atlas is away on business in the Antiarctic, Auntie Aspen has a tummy ache because of the baby, and Mommy had to go with Uncle Atlas so Uncle Royal is staying at her house—and then flops down in one of the chairs.

"Uncle Royal, I'm hungry," she says.

"Then it's time for us to go," he responds.

I reach out to gently stroke one of her soft, dark curls, thinking how beautiful she is. How smart and sweet and funny. Her mother and uncles must love her very much.

"Would you like me to sign something for you?" I ask her. "I don't have any pictures or anything with me."

"Uncle Royal, do we have the programmer?"

"The program," he corrects absently. "But no. We left it in Uncle Atlas's suite."

"Oh, I've got mine." I quickly get it out of my bag, where I'd stuffed it, and dig out a Sharpie. It's become habit to carry one with me everywhere so I sign the front of the program with lots of hearts and swirlies, and hand it to her.

She clutches it to her chest. "Thank you! I love it!"

"You're very welcome. Would you like to take a picture?"

"Can we, Uncle Royal? Since you writed a song together?"

"Wrote." We gently correct her in unison and, for the first time, our eyes meet.

His are shrouded and wary, which makes no sense since he's the one who snuck out like a thief in the night.

"Since you wrote a song together!" She claps her hands happily.

"I'll take it, Ms. Cantrell." Larry holds out his hand to Royal who looks at it blankly for a beat before opening his phone, typing in the passcode, and then handing it to him.

I get to my feet, and Royal comes to stand next to me.

Good-golly-Miss-Molly, just having the side of his arm brush against mine makes goosebumps break out on my flesh.

What the heck is wrong with me when it comes to this guy? He showed me that I was nothing more than a notch on his bedpost, so there is no reason for me to still get all tingly inside when he's near me.

Then the jerk puts his arm around me—the one with the hand that doesn't work properly—and I suspect it's to keep it hidden. The fingers curl a little when he's not using it, so I'm guessing he's self-conscious about it. I turn my body to a slight angle, further hiding his hand as Frankie stands up on the chair.

"We don't stand on furniture, Tater Tot," Royal says quietly.

She sighs dramatically and gets down. "But now I'm too short."

"I've got you, kiddo." I reach down and pick her up, settling her on the hip where Royal's bad hand is loosely resting.

He pulls it back.

Two birds, one metaphorical stone.

We take a bunch of pictures and then the crowd is in another uproar so I set Frankie down and she runs to the railing to see what's going on.

"A fight!" she exclaims. "It's Uncle Banks! Oh, no." She immediately covers her eyes.

"It's okay," I say, moving toward her without thinking. I pull her against my side and stroke her hair. "You must know it's part of the game and usually not real."

"I know," she whispers against my hip, "but it's *Uncle Banks*. Auntie Aspen doesn't like it when he fights either."

I bet.

"See, it's all done," I whisper several moments later, kneeling down again and hugging her. "And he's sitting in the penalty box, safe and sound."

"Okay." She lets out a little sigh of relief and drops her hands.

"We should go, Tater Tot. Ms. Cantrell has other people to talk to."

"She does?" Frankie looks around. "Who?"

I bite back a laugh. "It's okay," I tell Royal. "*She* can watch the game with me." I emphasize the word she just enough for him to get my meaning, hopefully without Frankie catching on.

"Yay! Can I, Uncle Royal? Pretty please with sugar and sprinkles on top?"

His lips thin, annoyance practically seeping out of him, but it's gone almost as quickly as it came. "We have to go, Tater Tot. We've taken enough of Ms. Cantrell's time. I'm sure she's *very busy* writing new songs."

I frown.

Was that a jab of some kind?

Why is he acting like I'm the one who did something wrong?

"Larry," I say, "would you get Frankie some fresh popcorn?"

"Absolutely." He nods and slips out.

Frankie's immersed in the game and I lower my voice as I move closer to Royal. "You can leave her here until the end of the game. I don't mind."

He shakes his head. "She's my responsibility, which means I don't let her out of my sight."

"Okay. I just thought it might be fun for her. You're welcome to stay as well. It's not like we have to talk."

He snorts. "Yeah, you did all your talking to the press."

"*Excuse* me?" It's hard to keep my voice down, but I somehow manage.

"Apparently, we're writing new songs together," he says dryly. "Anything to keep your name associated with mine, eh?"

My mouth falls open, and I stare at him. "I'm sorry—*I'm* not the one who was caught sneaking out of my hotel room early the morning after..." I don't finish my sentence. "And maybe that kind of thing is an everyday occurrence for you, but it's not for me. I have a reputation to uphold. I *care* what people think of me."

We stare at each other and I see the wheels turning.

"There were pictures?" he asks finally.

I give him a look. "Oh, so you know all about what I said about us working on new music but not that you were seen leaving my room? Or how I got ambushed by a reporter and I had to think fast because my former publicist couldn't be bothered to pay attention?" I grind my teeth together then exhale, trying to keep hold of my temper. "And anyway, I didn't say we *were* writing music, I simply said people would have to wait and find out."

His eyes burn into mine. "Which is essentially the same thing."

I shrug. "That's not my problem. I had to do damage control on the fly. Otherwise, not only did we spend the night together, you snuck out like I was nothing more than another one-night stand. Which is fine—except for the part where it makes me look like some trashy bimbo who meant nothing to you." For some reason, my eyes feel a little scratchy and I turn to watch what's going on out on the ice.

Darn it.

Why do I want to cry?

"Wait. No." He runs a hand through his hair. "That's not... shit. I—" He's interrupted as the crowd erupts once again, and this time, it's Banks who scores.

I keep my gaze on Frankie as she dances around the suite happily, completely ignoring us.

"I didn't know," Royal says once things have settled down again and his voice is softer. "For that, I'm sorry. I thought..."

"I know what you thought," I say when he doesn't finish. "But that's not me. And I don't need to link my name to yours. My name does just fine on its own. Yes, you wrote that song, but I'm the one who made it a hit. The bulk of my fan base are country music fans—they don't know who Royal Ewing is. And they don't care."

He looks like I slapped him.

Dang it.

I take a moment to gently backpedal.

"I just mean, country music fans don't necessarily follow a rock guitarist like Royal Ewing—they follow Jade Cantrell."

"Until you told the world that we were writing a song *together*," he grumbles. "Now they're following both of us."

I lift my chin. "I did what I had to do. Just like you did the morning after our night together."

"Except now we have to figure out what to do about it."

"We don't. We can just say we didn't have time in our schedules and eventually everyone will forget all about it."

His eyes settle on mine and whatever is lurking beneath those blue depths is hard to read.

He takes what feels like a long time to respond, his jaw working the entire time.

"We could...make the time."

I frown.

"But it has to be on my terms," he adds in a rush, as though he can't believe he's actually saying what he's saying. "And it can't be in L.A."

My heart starts pounding.

"I—"

"I know a place that's private," he says. "No press. No pictures. Just music."

"I don't know if I have time," I admit despite the excitement building in my chest.

I *want* to spend time with him again.

Even if it's platonic.

Well, it absolutely has to be platonic.

I'm not doing *that* again. Nope, no way. It's far too dangerous for me.

But the lure of actually writing a song, *together*, is more than I can resist.

"It wouldn't take long," he says, those deep-set eyes boring into mine. "Three or four days at most."

I open my mouth. Close it again. That's hardly any time at all. Three days is totally doable.

Right?

"It can only be business," I say with as much certainty as I can muster up.

"Absolutely." He's waiting for a response, eyes never leaving mine.

Jiminy crickets.

This is going to be a huge mistake.

But I'm going to do it.

I can't help myself.

So, I take a breath, jump right into the deep end, and just say, "Give me the details."

CHAPTER ELEVEN

Royal

I PULL my rental SUV to a stop in front of the secluded resort and pop open the door, drawing in my first full breath in what feels like an eternity.

The crisp winter air, the dusting of snow on the conifers, the deep blue waters of the lake visible in the distance.

Tahoe is a special place, and it never fails to settle me.

I wish it was closer to southern California, and yeah, yeah, I know all the SoCal natives will say that we have Mammoth, but it's not the same as…

I inhale again.

It's not the same as *here.*

I unbuckle and hop out, moving over to the porch of the main house to meet Dave, who runs the place.

I'll grab the keys for both cabins—a pair that's farthest away from the rest—and get everything ready for Jade when her driver drops her off.

She's busier than I am, Hollywood wanting their piece of her now that she's the hottest thing on the planet, and she's still struggling to find the balance of yes and no.

Of course, for me that default is set at no and *more* no.

Easier that way.

"Royal," Dave says, extending his hand for me to shake.

I do, even as I hate the reminder of my accident.

Dulled sensation, fingers that struggle to work, far too much focus to complete a simple task I never used to think about.

"Good to see you," I tell him before I pull back. "I appreciate the favor. I know this place is booked up this time of year."

A shrug of his flannel-covered shoulders.

This is a man who thrives in the outdoors, who hikes and snowboards and boats, who chops wood and scares off bears with only his bare—no pun intended—hands and shovels driveways.

He's not afraid of hard work, is down to earth, and lives a simple life.

And running this place helps him keep doing that.

Especially now that he caters to the wealthy.

"I'm just glad we had that cancelation and could accommodate you." He claps me on the shoulder. "You know I love having you here."

I smirk. "Just not enough to kick out another paying customer."

He taps his nose. "Got it in one." A tilt of his head to the door of the main house. "I'll just run in for the key. Want a cup of coffee for the road?"

"Just the keys," I tell him.

He nods and disappears inside, the door slamming behind him.

I turn to soak in the view of the valley, the granite mountains and the rows and rows of pine trees. The lake that draws everyone in, the narrow stretch of beach that's not, by any stretch of the imagination, warm, even in the middle of summer.

The door opens behind me, and I rotate back to face Dave as he comes out with an envelope and keys.

"I warned your assistant when she called to make the reservation, that there's a big storm coming in. It might take a few days for the roads to be cleared enough to get back to the airport."

I look up, see that the sky is a dark gray and, yeah, the air's cool enough to indicate snow, but everything's so carefully manicured here—trails designed to look natural, but someone would have to be a complete idiot to not be able to follow, along with heated driveways and carefully sloped roads—that I've never felt anything but safe and comfortable.

A little snow?

All the better.

It means more people will stay away.

And a few days is perfect—make some music, scratch this perpetual itch that Jade has created in me, and go back to normal.

"We'll have power, though," he says, "every cabin has a generator if the lines go down and plenty of firewood. I even checked that the cabin's fireplaces were ready to roll."

"That works for us," I say. "Less distractions and more time writing music."

"Can't wait to hear it." He passes over the keys and envelope. "I'm sure it'll be just as big as 'Forever in Rewind.'" A grin. "That shit's catchy as hell."

I snort. "Well, I'll take my streaming residuals all the way to the bank."

"Damn right you will." Another clap on my shoulder before he nods at the hillside. "I put you in cabin six as usual."

The farthest away from the others.

Perfect.

"And the other cabin's five?"

There's a blip of quiet that has my stomach sinking.

"Other cabin?"

Yeah, that sends the sinking...*sinking* further. And adding some knots alongside it.

"We asked for two cabins," I say slowly.

Dave's brows shoot up. "Royal, man." His words are quiet, but firm and confident. "I took the call from your assistant myself. She asked for one cabin—which I could accommodate. If she'd asked for two, I couldn't have done that. We're full and everyone's hunkering down, getting ready to enjoy the snow and quiet."

Fuck.

"There are no other cancelations?" I ask. "Not even here at the main house?"

He shakes his head. "That could change, but I doubt it. You're the last one to check in."

A throb pulses through my temple. "Shit," I mutter. "This isn't what we planned. I promised Jade—"

Curiosity slides across his face, and I shake myself.

What the fuck am I doing saying that shit out loud?

Being a goddamned idiot is what.

I open my mouth to spin some bullshit, but he beats me to a reply.

"I'll let you know if anything changes." Steady eyes on mine. "And if push comes to shove, you can sleep on my couch."

The tangle of my insides loosens.

Dave's a good guy.

"Not offering to share your bed with me?" I say lightly.

He snorts. "You pretentious Hollywood types are never satisfied, are you? I offer my couch and *only* my couch." His mouth twitches. "You want in my bed, you'd at least have to buy me dinner first."

"Noted," I mutter.

He grins. "Shoot me a text or call with any problems."

"Like one cabin instead of two?" I can't help but saying.

He winces. "I'll make it up to you next time you're here."

Nodding, I head back to my SUV and start to get in just as I see the black sedan head up the road. Catching the driver's eyes, I indicate that he follow me, and hop in, winding through the trees until we get to my usual cabin.

I park, grab my bag from the trunk, then wait as they pull in beside me.

"Hey," I say to John, remembering him (and his discretion) from the after party a couple weeks back.

"Mr. Ewing," he replies, pulling open the back door for Jade before heading to the trunk.

And then…

She's climbing out of the car.

Fuck.

She's wearing jeans and a sweater, her hair piled up on top of her head—

And yet she's more beautiful than when she'd been all dolled up at the awards.

Though, certainly not more beautiful than when she'd been naked and coming on my cock.

Her cheeks flush when she realizes that I'm watching her, and I hate the uncertainty that creeps into her eyes, hate it enough that I remind my cock that this retreat isn't about sex.

It's about finding all the reasons to not want her, and to give her enough that those pictures don't follow her.

"Hey," she says, spinning in a circle and sighing softly. "This is a beautiful place."

"One of the best," I agree.

We're quiet for a moment, and I wonder if it's going to always be like this—tinged with awkwardness, with my mistakes.

If the chemistry from that night, the hours' long conversations that felt like seconds, are gone forever.

But then she turns to me, her smile small, her expression content, and I feel both in my cock, wrapping slender fingers around me, squeezing firmly, and pumping.

Jesus.

I shove that down, open my mouth to tell her about the problem with the cabins.

"I put your bags on the porch, Ms. Cantrell," John says. "Will there be anything else?"

"No," she says and I don't miss her passing him a folded bill. "Enjoy your vacation and I'll see you in a few days."

He nods. "I'll be in town if you need anything."

"Thanks," she murmurs, and then John's in the car, turning around and driving away.

Leaving us alone.

And leaving me to break the news.

And no, don't ask me why I didn't tell her before her ride left—that would involve me having to examine the bullshit in my head far too closely.

"Where's *your* cabin?" she asks softly.

"I—" Well, fuck, there's no easing into this, is there?

She frowns at my hesitation. "What is it?"

"There was a problem with the cabins." I explain about Briar's mistake making the reservation and Dave telling me the resort is full up. "So…" I clear my throat. "We only have one cabin."

Her eyes go wide as she squeaks. *"One?"*

Fuck, she's cute.

But I focus and nod in confirmation. "Yeah," I say. "But there are two bedrooms. We'll keep it strictly to music. I promise."

Her expression tells me that she doesn't buy this in the least.

"I'm really sorry. I didn't plan this, I swear."

Gray eyes study mine for a long, tense moment before she sighs.

"Fine," she mutters, pushing past me and bounding up the stairs to the cabin. "But there will absolutely be *no* hanky-panky."

CHAPTER TWELVE

Jade

ONE CABIN.

How do I get myself into these messes?

I should know better.

I don't know if I believe it was a mistake—people like Royal don't have assistants who make mistakes—but there are two bedrooms. And the lock on the door seems to work. Not that I'm afraid of him. Not physically anyway.

I look around the room, where I've unpacked my toiletries and pajamas and a few things I'll need to be comfortable in the next couple of days. It's beautiful. High-end rustic with large windows and warm furnishings.

In a way, it reminds me of my farmhouse in Tennessee. I've done all the renovations, updating and upgrading, making it a veritable paradise without losing the original charm. Yes, there are stainless steel appliances in the kitchen now—sorry, grandma, but that green 1970s look was unbearable—and granite countertops, along with a shower in my bathroom I could hold a party in.

I've made it mine and I miss it when I'm away, but being here reminds me of home.

Except, I'm not home and I have things to do.

With a sigh, I gather my courage and every drop of professionalism I can muster up, and head into the main room. It's expansive, with two-story ceilings and a floor-to-ceiling fireplace that would be perfect to cuddle in front of.

Ugh.

Stop it, Jade.

There will be no cuddling. None. Zero. Zip. Nada.

I repeat it until I kinda sorta believe it.

Then I step into the living room, and my resolve melts almost as fast as my panties the night of the award show.

Because Royal is the kind of man any red-blooded woman would want to cuddle with.

And I'm sure he has. Many, many times.

The devil on my shoulder is a jerk, and I take a breath before pasting a fake smile on my face. "Hey. Is there food?"

"Sure." He turns slowly, his eyes zeroing in on me like he's undressing me.

Is that what he's doing?

I resist the urge to cross my arms over my chest and walk toward the kitchen.

"What do you feel like?" he asks, following me.

"Just a snack to tide me over until dinner."

"I've got a chef coming to cook every night."

"Yes, I saw the menu you sent. Everything sounds delicious." I open the fridge, anxious for something to keep my hands busy.

Grapes.

Easy. Fast. I can just pop some in my mouth, which gives me something to do other than worry about how much I want him to touch me.

"So, do you have thoughts on what you want to work on?"

"I do," I admit, releasing an internalized breath I've been holding.

Music is safe territory.

"I've got some things I've been playing with that the record company wouldn't let me pursue, but now that I hold more power, I'm going to go with it. Do you, uh, want to hear?" I'm suddenly nervous.

This is *Royal Ewing.*

Yes, I'm a star, but I'm known for my voice, not my songwriting.

He was at least a co-writer for every single one of Midnight Sun's hits, so that's a little intimidating.

"Of course. That's why we're here." He plucks a grape off the bunch and pops it in his mouth, leaning a hip against the island. Why is he infuriatingly sexy? So much so that I'm having trouble concentrating on anything but the body I know is hidden beneath his jeans and long-sleeve Henley.

"Hang on." I hurry into the bedroom and grab my acoustic guitar.

How the hell am I going to play it in front of one of the premier guitar virtuoso's of our generation? He may not be able to play anymore but that doesn't negate who he is—was?—or his skill and musical IQ.

But I'm no slouch.

I'm a star too.

I remind myself of that as I walk back into the room where Royal is waiting on the couch, the bowl of grapes on the coffee table in front of him.

I lean on the edge of a nearby armchair and rest the guitar in my lap. "I call this one 'Remembering Never.' I don't have a chorus yet, just the first stanza, but the opening melody makes me happy."

I move my hands into position and slowly strum the opening bars. The strings are worn and comfortable against the pads of my fingers, like an old friend. I've had it since I was thirteen. It's the first guitar I ever owned and it's the only one I use when I'm writing. It's like working with an old friend.

You were never gonna love me

We were never gonna steal

Kisses in the night and the things that lovers feel.

You were never gonna take me

Or make me someone's wife

We were never gonna make it in this thing we call life.

I stop abruptly, since I haven't gotten much further. "I know, it's rough."

"It's not." He gives a small shake of his head. "Play the first part again."

I start over but before I start to sing, he stops me.

"A minor seventh there," he instructs. "And maybe this." He comes to stand behind me, covering my left hand with his, showing me the chords he has in mind.

And of course, it's brilliant.

Exactly what the song needs.

He's so good.

We play around with lyrics and melody for the next hour, with him guiding me on the guitar as I find the soul of the song.

Why is it so easy with him?

It's like he breathes the music. It's part of him, and despite my ongoing irritation with how he walked out on me, my heart breaks a little too. The weight of what he lost is never as tangible as it is in this room, right now, and I just want to hug him. Kiss him. Somehow make it all better.

I know I can't.

Nothing can.

But I desperately want to.

And it's reflected in the lyrics we write, even if neither of us wants to acknowledge it.

Stolen moments, cold as sin

Remember to never do this again.

Heartbreaking aura, skin on skin,

This is all we have

Remember baby—never again.

"I like this," he murmurs.

His tone is gruff, heavy, almost the same voice he used when was inside of me.

Good gracious, what am I doing?

I feel a little flushed with him leaning over me, his left hand covering mine and occasionally taking over the fret work. It's hard to concentrate when he's so close, the scruff of his beard occasionally brushing against my cheek. Having him this close is intoxicating, no matter how many times I tell my traitorous body he's bad news.

My body only remembers the good things. The orgasms. The kisses that rocked my world. The caresses that made me feel more alive than anything other than being on stage.

I'm so lost in my memories of our night together that my fingers fumble over the chords, I can't remember the lyrics we just added, and I stop abruptly.

"Sugar biscuits," I mutter, shaking my head. "I don't know what…I'm sorry."

"It's all right." His tone is as gentle as the hand resting on my shoulder. "We can start over."

"I just…" I lift my gaze to find his mouth inches from mine.

And the world stops.

I'm momentarily…mesmerized.

Oh no.

This is *bad*.

"I want…uh, I don't think…" Why can't I form a sentence?

Probably because those gorgeous blue eyes are filled with raw, unadulterated desire.

No-no-no.

We have a deal.

This is just work.

"It's really good," he says softly, that darn hand still resting on my shoulder, bringing warmth to regions much farther south. "We're close."

Yes. Yes, we are.

"We, uh, work well together," I say instead.

"We do. Our musical styles mesh."

"I like working with you," I whisper. I know I shouldn't have, but it slips out before I can stop it. Professionally speaking, there's no reason to lie. The problem is I'm talking about more than work and we both know it.

"It feels easy," he agrees. "Like we've done it before."

Like something *else* we've done before.

That was easy too.

Until it wasn't.

"I've never co-written a song with anyone," I say. "I thought it would be...harder." If there's innuendo in there, he doesn't react.

He just keeps watching me with those gorgeous blue eyes.

I distinctly remember what it was like having those eyes burning into mine while he moved inside of me. As he kissed and nipped and caressed every inch of me. But it's the moment just before he came, his body covering mine, that I think of most. The way he looked at me, as if I was his everything.

No one has ever looked at me like that.

It wasn't real, though.

Nothing but a stolen moment in time.

Oh good grief, is that where that lyric came from?

My memories of our lovemaking?

Crap on a cracker.

This is going to be a disaster.

And yet, his face is still dangerously close to mine.

His lips…

He hasn't moved away.

And someone has to.

Before we do something stupid.

He leans closer and panic wells up inside of me.

I *cannot* do this again.

I want to so much, but I know better.

"Royal…no. We can't—" I stand up abruptly, almost dropping my guitar as I run toward the front door.

"Jade!" I hear him call my name, but I can't stop moving until I'm as far away from him as possible.

Until I can breathe again.

Being in the same room as Royal Ewing is suffocating. He's the kind of guy who can hurt me.

And I plan to avoid that at all costs.

Even if the cost is my heart.

CHAPTER THIRTEEN

Royal

I GIVE HER SPACE.

I know I owe her at least that much, considering how close I came to kissing her.

Except, I promised no hanky-panky.

My lips twitch because her whole no saying naughty words thing is cute as hell, but just as quickly, my smile fades.

Because I promised no sex.

And it took me all of a couple of hours to almost break that promise.

Fucking asshole.

That's me, in case it wasn't obvious.

Groaning, I shove the last of the food into the fridge then study the menu on the counter, wondering how in the hell I'm going to pull off dinner.

It's simple cuisine—because I don't have the patience for pretentious bullshit—but it's also completely out of my wheelhouse.

I don't cook. Unless boxed pasta and jarred sauce and some of those breadsticks that come in a can count. And, in this case, they don't. There's fresh tomatoes and mozzarella, a container of homemade pasta that needs to be cooked.

But no cans or jars in sight.

And apparently, we no longer have a chef coming in.

He dropped off the bags of food while I was giving Jade "space" and told me that the storm will prevent him from driving out to cook for us.

Speaking of which, it's getting dark, the stormfront drawing close.

I need to go and find her.

I snag my jacket from the hooks by the front door, shove my feet into my boots, and hope to hell that she isn't going to prove my earlier thought about it being nearly impossible to get lost on the resort wrong.

There's one path that leads off from the cabin, and I follow it, searching for any sign of her, and heart sinking when I don't find anything for several long minutes.

But then I round a gentle corner and see footprints in a patch of snow.

Fresh prints.

Made by small feet.

Thank fuck.

I pick up my pace, listening intently, gaze searching, but it takes another five minutes for me to spot the blond of her hair amongst the trees.

She's sitting on a boulder, her legs bent, her chin resting on the tops of her knees, her arms banded around her shins.

She paints a lonely picture, sitting up there like that, all by herself, and my pace slows as I take in the sight of her, as I drink in the ethereal image she makes. Need burns through me—to climb on behind her and wrap her in my arms, to lift her hair to the side and kiss her nape, to strip her naked and fuck her on that rock.

I'd deal with the cold and let her ride me.

My lips twitch as I move closer—oh the humanity, oh the

sacrifice of having to be beneath Jade as she rides me to completion, those tits bouncing, her pussy a hot clasp around my dick…

I'd survive.

Just barely.

I start to make my way to the front of the boulder when I'm close enough to notice something I've missed—and it's something that eliminates every ounce of amusement I've been feeling.

She's shivering.

Fuck, I'm lusting after her like a teenage boy and she's…cold and alone and—

"Jade," I say quietly, not wanting to startle her.

She jumps anyway, whipping around on the rock and promptly losing her balance.

I lunge toward her, snaking an arm around her body, catching her before she tumbles from the boulder.

It's not graceful in the least, and even though my arm is around her shoulders, it's really my body that's keeping her from falling.

"R-Royal," she stammers.

And I know.

I feel it too.

She's pinned between my body and the rock, our fronts pressed together, and—

My dick twitches, something I know she feels because her eyes go wide and she mutters, "Fiddlesticks."

Cute.

Too fucking cute.

"Sorry I scared you," I murmur, adjusting my grip so I can lower her to the ground.

Slowly, so I don't drop her, I allow her front to drag along mine, inch by torturous inch…and loving every second of the contact.

Yes, I'm a pervert.

No, I can't stop myself.

When she finally has her feet beneath her, I shift back enough so that I can slip my coat off.

"What are—"

But she doesn't finish the question because I'm shifting again, this time to wrap my jacket around her.

"You're cold," I say softly.

"I'm fine," she whispers back.

"You're trembling." I reach for the buttons and do them up. "And only wearing that thin shirt."

It's long-sleeved, but clearly not doing much to protect her from the elements or the storm coming in.

Her eyes drift to mine, and she studies me for several long moments before quietly asking, "Why did you come find me?"

She's trembling so hard, even with my jacket, that I grind my teeth together and clench my hands into fists—the good one anyway, the useless, fucked-up one only creates a loose approximation of something that resembles a fist. I shove that thought away, resist the urge to draw her close, to wrap my arms around her, to rub my hands up and down her back, warming her so she stops shivering.

"You were gone a while," I say, tilting my head down the path. "I was worried."

"I was fine."

"I know," I tell her as we start walking, wondering how often she reassures the people around her that she's fine…

And how often she really isn't.

Focus.

"But I need to talk to you about the storm that's coming in." I point up at the gray sky, the dark, almost black clouds creeping along the horizon in the distance. "Everyone's saying it's supposed to be a bad one"—I glance down at her—"so much so that roads might be closed."

Her brows lift. "But don't they have plows and stuff?"

I nod. "They do. But Dave—the owner of the resort," I explain when confusion drifts across her fact, "says they might take a couple of days to clear everything enough for us to be out of here."

She's quiet for a moment then shrugs. "Well, that's fine. We're planning on holing up and writing music, not sightseeing."

"True." I glance down at her. "Full disclosure?"

"Yes. Please."

"Dave told me that each cabin has a generator, so we'll have power if it goes out. And there's plenty of firewood, so we'll have heat."

"That doesn't sound so bad."

I nod in agreement. "We also have food because the chef dropped it off…" And here's the part that might have her calling her driver back so she can get the fuck out of here. "Right before he told me he won't be back during our stay because he doesn't think he'll be able to safely make it back until the storm passes and the road's clear."

"Having food also isn't a bad thing," she says as we round the corner and the cabin comes into sight, her brows furrowing into a vee I'm suddenly desperate to kiss.

"You'd think so," I say dryly as we approach the front door. "But that's before you've had my cooking."

Her mouth quirks.

"So," I say before she can reply, "if you want to abandon this weekend and try for another time so you're not stuck here with me, I wouldn't blame you."

She pauses with her hand on the knob then glances up at me. "Something like this isn't easy to reschedule."

"No, it isn't." I nudge her out of the way and open the door, shepherding her inside. "But I know your schedule's packed and if there's a chance that we won't get out of here on time because of the storm…"

She pauses in the hall, fingers fiddling with the buttons on my coat. "Then we'd have time to write even more music."

But the words are lacking confidence.

And I know that's because of me.

"About before…"

She stops fiddling.

"I shouldn't have done that—" Storm cloud gray eyes fly to mine and my heart skips a beat, knowing that I'm going to write some lyrics about her gorgeous eyes—hell, maybe I'll pen an entire song or album or a fucking Iliad-length epic poem about them. Just…not right now. "I promised you this would just be work," I say, "and I broke that promise."

She sucks in a breath.

"I'm sorry."

She's quiet for an eternity—a torturously long eternity.

"No bullshit," I say into the silence. Because I owe her at least that much. "It won't happen again. I'll make certain of that."

More quiet in response.

More torturous silence.

More stormy gray eyes.

But then she seems to unstick, her fingers working on the buttons on my coat again—this time to undo them before she slips the material from her shoulders and hangs it onto the hook.

"Right then," she says, brushing her hands together. "Should we get back to work?"

CHAPTER FOURTEEN

Jade

I WAKE TO A CRACKLING SOUND.

The fireplace.

I'm warm and comfy and—*wait.*

There's no fireplace in my room.

My eyes pop open, and the first thing I see is Royal, bent over, stoking the fire. And his ass—covered by loose gray sweats—looks good enough to take a bite out of.

I blink and rub my eyes.

"What time is it?" I ask in a voice still raspy from sleep.

"Just after nine in the morning."

"When did..." I look down and note that I'm covered in a warm fleece blanket, a pillow tucked under my head.

"You fell asleep while we were talking," he said, finally standing up straight and turning around. "You looked so comfortable, I grabbed a blanket and just let you sleep."

Why does he have to be so sweet when he wants to be?

If he would just be a jerk all the time, it would be easier.

"I need to freshen up," I murmur, swinging my legs over the edge and sitting up.

"I brewed a pot of coffee, so we can have breakfast whenever you're ready. And I want to show you something I've been working on."

"Okay." My phone is still on the coffee table and as I stand up, my ringtone plays the theme to "Hawaii Five-0," Farrah's name flashing on the screen.

Firing her has turned into a whole situation that I'm sick of.

I press the button to send the call to voicemail, scowling at the screen.

"Someone can't take no for an answer," I mutter.

"What's going on?" Royal asks quietly since he's probably close enough to see who was calling.

"I fired my publicist, but my management company uses her for all of their artists so they're pushing back."

"Why did you fire her?"

I hesitate. "Well…because of you, I guess."

"Because of me?" He looks confused.

"When Liza Bancroft blindsided me during that interview, talking about how you were seen leaving my hotel room, asking whether or not we were sleeping together, all that stuff—Farrah just sat there playing on her phone. Then, when I confronted her in the car afterward, she basically blew me off and downplayed it." I hesitate, not wanting to let him know how much I think about him, but I also feel like it's important to be honest. About this anyway. "I remembered what you told me about making sure I surround myself with people I trust. And I don't trust her anymore. So I fired her."

He's quiet for a moment, watching me intently. "You did the right thing. But now you have to man up, so to speak, and stick to your guns. Don't let them tell you who you have to work with. You have the power now, Jade."

"Sometimes it doesn't feel like it." I stare into the fireplace, watching the flames dance and swirl. "Sometimes I feel like a puppet being pulled in so many directions I get dizzy."

"I remember that feeling well. But at some point, you have to put yourself first."

"How expensive do you think it'll be for me to break all ties?" I ask softly. It's almost rhetorical because I don't think there's any way for him to know. I didn't even realize that was in the back of my mind until the words slipped out.

"It shouldn't cost you anything," he says. "If they care about public perception, they'll let you go. But you should get a good lawyer and say that there are creative differences now that you've gotten to this point in your career. It depends on the specifics of your contract, but honestly, you should be able to get out of it. They could fight you, and they probably will, but I can recommend a badass entertainment attorney who can help you with this. If you want to talk to her, I'll send you her info."

"Yes. Thank you."

"Any time." He nods for the hall. "You were going to go freshen up?"

"Oh, right." I hurry into my room.

I look a little tired, and my hair's in a messy ponytail, but that's okay. The less attractive I am, the less chance there will be that we almost kiss again. Last night, he was on his best behavior —so much so it's almost insulting considering that my body is in a constant state of arousal. Just being in the same room as him makes it hard to think.

The good news is that he's a masterful songwriter and we genuinely work well together. We feed off each other's ideas, and though I'm nowhere near the guitar player he was, he does it all by ear. He can tell me what chords to play—and he's right on. Every. Single. Time. It's unnerving how instinctive it is for him.

"What's for breakfast?" I ask when I find him in the kitchen.

"There's a quiche and the instructions look pretty simple. I preheated the oven, so we should be good to go in about twenty-five minutes."

"Perfect. Let me get some coffee, and you can show me what you were talking about."

"Great." He leaves the kitchen as I pour myself a cup of coffee.

It's been snowing since last night and everything is coated in white. Even though it's somewhat dark and gloomy, it's also mystical and beautiful and inspiring. I want to write a song about it. But not just the snow. I want to capture the whole feeling, the essence of the snow. Or the essence of being snowed in with a gorgeous stranger.

"Midnight snow," I murmur, immediately pulling my phone out of my pocket.

"Midnight snow?" Royal asks, startling me.

"Song title," I say, holding up my cell. "I make notes in my phone."

"Jesus, you're like a fucking mind reader," he says.

"What do you mean?" I ask absently as I type in my thoughts.

"Last night, after you fell asleep, I was thinking the same thing. Not midnight snow, specifically—I kind of hate the word midnight, if you know what I mean—but just snow that falls at night. How it looks as it's coming down and the feelings it inspires."

"Oh." I look up, finding his strong gaze zeroed in on mine. "I'm sorry about the word midnight, but it works for me. For this."

"It does." He scratches his head. "Anyway, I brought your guitar. I worked on some lyrics while I was watching the snow fall, and I have some melodies in my head. If you can play this series of chords…" He hands me a piece of paper.

It looks simple enough, so I nod and perch on the end of one of the stools. The music comes almost naturally, as if I already know the melody.

Because he's singing it.

And though it's not exactly what I had in mind, it's in the same vein.

As if we really can read each other's minds.

"*Midnight,*" he sings, his voice deep and rich. "*When there's no one but you and me, girl. Snowfall, like an avalanche of pearls. Come and show me…la-di-da-midnight…*"

"Oh, yes. Yes!" I immediately pick it up. "*…it feels like morning but it's barely midnight, you and me, boy, not lettin' you out of my sight…*" I cut off abruptly, glance over at him. "A duet."

He frowns. "I don't sing. I mean, not like that. I'm not a lead singer."

"But you could do part of this one. I can carry us, and you have no problem harmonizing…Look." I hand him the guitar and run into the living room where we left the notebooks we'd been doodling in all day yesterday.

He follows me, thoughtfully carrying both my guitar and the mug of coffee I'd already forgotten about.

I'm writing furiously on one of the pads, rough lyrics practically pouring out of me.

THERE'S *no time like midnight when it's snowing*
I look in your eyes, baby, you're glowing
Show me the moon and I'll give you the stars
Baby, you know me, and this night is ours.

HE NODS, humming along.

"*Baby, you're glowing…*" he sings. "That would be my verse."

Then he's beside me, watching as I write. "No, what about 'this time is ours' instead of 'this night'?"

That could work. I scribble the new lyrics, decide I don't like them, and go back to the original.

The oven timer goes off, alerting us that breakfast is ready, and I reluctantly put down the guitar.

"Let's pick this up after we eat," I suggest.

"Sure." He follows me into the kitchen.

My phone goes off again, and I roll my eyes before sending it to voicemail and setting it on the counter.

"Farrah again?" he asks.

"No, my manager. They want to schedule a video conference call to discuss what happened. Farrah is apparently quite contrite, apologizing all over the place—she even sent me flowers. I'm just not interested."

"Tell them that. And this is truly your way out."

"What do you mean?" I ask, taking the quiche out of the oven.

"You get a good lawyer to say they aren't representing your best interests. Document everything. Sit down right now, while we're having breakfast, and make notes. Exactly what happened with Farrah, the date, as close to the time as you remember… you're 'in the studio' this weekend working on new music and they're bombarding you with annoying calls. Use anything and everything, Jade." He sounds so sincere, I'm momentarily emotional.

"I will. Thank you." I go get my notebook and bring it back to the kitchen, jotting down the dates and times I can remember Farrah not doing her job, and digging through my email for the approved list of questions for that interview with Liza Bancroft.

Royal eats quietly while I make notes, letting me get it all down.

This is good stuff, things I wouldn't have thought to do on my own.

He's a royal pain-in-the-butt, but I'm starting to see the man beneath the rough façade.

And despite my best efforts not to, I'm starting to like him even more.

CHAPTER FIFTEEN

Royal

SHE HUMS as she stirs the pot, hips swaying, hair having slipped from the holder to skate down her back.

Blond strands spread out on a pillow behind her head while she was naked beneath me.

Falling into her face as I'd fucked her from behind.

Long enough to hold on to when—

"Can you check and see if the chef left some basil?" she asks absently.

I tear my gaze from her ass, which is encased in a pair of tight jeans. Her feet are bare, her toes painted a pale pink that matches the color of her lips. Of *both* lips—

"Royal?" she prompts.

I shake myself. "Yeah," I say gruffly as I go to the fridge. But after staring at the contents for near on a minute, I have to admit, "What does basil look like?"

Her giggle is like a fucking ray of sunlight, so bright that I'm nearly blinded.

Or maybe it's the contact of her body against mine as she nudges me out of the way. "When you said you didn't cook..."

"I meant I didn't cook," I say, my voice more than a little rough. "Briar, my assistant," I add when Jade's brows pull together, "is in charge of cooking when I eat food that's not take out or something frozen my chef left for me to reheat."

Like the quiche this morning.

"I'm excellent at peeling potatoes," I add hopefully.

Her lips quirk. "I'll keep that in mind."

"Damn right, you will."

Another of those giggles I want to taste on my tongue, the bright humor I want to bask in. I've been in the shadows for so fucking long…

Pain and numbness. Loneliness but unable to let anyone close, not even my family. A gnawing ache because—

I grind my teeth together.

Because I lost my purpose.

Fucking pathetic.

I'm rich. Famous. Have so much privilege I'm practically drowning in it. The last thing anyone needs to be concerned about is me being unhappy.

I'm fine.

"I'll look for the basil," Jade murmurs and nods to the pot. "You go stir the sauce."

"On it," I say, doing just that. "What are you making, anyway?"

"My grandma's famous—or at least, famous to me, marinara sauce." She closes the fridge and holds up something green and leafy—that I presume to be basil—up. "We're not Italian." A shrug. "But it was one of my favorite things she cooked."

"What were some of the others?" I ask, genuinely interested in what makes this woman tick.

Music. A farm in Tennessee. Marinara sauce. Coffee.

"Lemon drizzle cake," she says. "And popcorn balls. Chicken 'n dumplin's." A sigh. "The absolute best scalloped potatoes and meatloaf you would have ever tasted."

"You miss her."

She settles the basil on the cutting board, starts tearing the leaves into chunks that she adds to the sauce. "Yeah," she murmurs. "My parents…well, *she* was my parent, for all intents and purposes. I was so young when I lost my dad, and then losing my mom…" Her throat works. "I needed her a lot then, and my grandma stepped in."

"I'm glad you had that," I tell her.

Her gaze slides to mine, face gentling. "And you didn't?"

I freeze. "I just know a little bit about parents who weren't all that great at parenting is all."

Her eyes soften further. "What does that mean?"

I shrug. "Usual shit. Toxic people. Extra toxic together. My dad was a serial cheater and workaholic. My mom shopped her feelings away."

"Did they ever get divorced?"

I shake my head. "Nope. They were still together till the end, still living to make each other miserable."

"They're gone now?"

"Mom to cancer. Dad to a heart attack," I say. "And maybe it makes me an asshole, but it was a relief, in a way, when they were gone. No more phone calls bitching about each other. No more drama. No more mistresses to pay off for my dad or credit cards for my mom. My real family is far more peaceful."

She snags the spoon from me, takes over stirring, and is quiet for a long moment. "What do you mean, your *real* family?"

"I firmly believe that you can pick the people you deem family."

More stirring.

"You disagree?" I ask.

The spoon pauses, and she glances up at me with those gorgeous gray eyes. "No," she says slowly. "Not exactly. I just…I just never really thought about it that way, I guess. But with my grandma being gone and Farrah doing what she did, I just realized I don't have a bio family, and I don't have a work one either."

My cold, dead heart squeezes. "You have the chance to make your own. Get people around you who you trust. Connect with those who fulfill you." I wink at her, hating to see the sadness in her eyes. "Maybe find someone who can make a really good marinara?"

The corners of her mouth turn up. "Is that how you made yours?"

"Nope," I say, "I was dragged kicking and screaming into my family."

She laughs, but it sounds as though it's been torn out of her, the sad not completely erased from the corners of her expression, and maybe that's why I keep talking.

"I played hockey with the guys in college—Banks, who you saw when you went to the Vipers' game—"

She nods.

"He, Atlas, Dash, Colt, and I. We were really good together—though Banks was the best of us. It's why he made it to the NHL while the rest of us had to find other things to do."

Her smile this time is genuine, and it warms that place where her giggles touched earlier. "Other things to do *meaning*…being part of the biggest rock band on the planet, and"—she taps her bottom lip—"being friends with…Atlas Delarosa?"

I nod.

"The billionaire who has his hands in all sorts of successful companies?"

I grunt. "He's always been a show-off."

She grins. "I don't know a famous Dash though."

"He prefers it that way. Hudson—or Dash as they called him on the ice, a nickname that stuck—runs a security firm for the rich and famous."

"Handy." A strand of hair falls into her face, and I tuck it behind her ear.

I know I shouldn't.

But touching her—

Nope. Not going there.

"Definitely handy," I say. "He handles security for Banks, Atlas, and I as necessary, and has loads of other clients in Hollywood."

"Is it dangerous?"

"It can be."

She touches my shoulder. "You must worry about him."

"He's very good at his job."

"You still worry." She's not wrong, and I find that I can't lie to her.

"We all worry. After we lost Colt—"

She gasps, and I remember she couldn't know that.

"It was four years ago now," I tell her. "He and Dash were in the military. A mission went very wrong and Colt died. After… well, Dash was so cut up about it, we thought we'd lose him too. But we managed to find something to keep us together."

"What?"

"The Sapphire Room."

"That…sounds familiar."

"It's a private club down in L.A.," I explain. "Colt was a big partier, and he would have gotten a huge kick out of owning a club, especially one with a drink named after him."

Jade touches my arm. "That's really cool of you guys to do that."

A blip of guilt slides through me.

Because, yeah, I kicked in some money, but I haven't exactly been hands on. I've been relying on Atlas and Banks—and now, Aspen, since she became manager—to run the club. I need to pull my weight more, need to not be such a grumpy, useless asshole.

"Colt was important to us all," I tell her and hold up my arm, showing her the tattoo we all got memorializing him. "Each of the guys has this, albeit in different spots, and the club…" I exhale, the pain of losing him still almost excruciating. "We get together often, but we always make sure to do it on his birthday—to tie one on and drink Gamebreakers in his honor. There are girls and food and…" I shrug. "It's a tribute to him."

"That's beautiful," she murmurs.

"Yeah," I agree.

The quiet that falls between us isn't tense.

It's…contemplative.

At least until the pasta water almost boils over. Then Jade's snagging the pot, draining off the water. I step back as she dumps the pasta into the pot of sauce, stirring it so it's completely covered before handing me a loaf of French bread.

"Would you mind slicing this?" She scowls, swatting at that errant strand of hair that's escaped again.

She's cute as hell.

"Slicing is well within my skill set," I tell her as I take the bread.

A laugh. "Glad to hear it."

In short order, we've—well, *Jade*—has made up plates and I bring the bread and butter to the table. There's a container of salad in the fridge, so I snag that too so we can pretend to be healthy. But really, I've got my eye on the tiramisu.

The silence falls between us again, and I can't help but feel…

Well, like sandpaper has been rubbed along my skin.

Raw and a little vulnerable.

I don't talk about this shit with people.

Let alone with people I barely know.

And here I am, spilling my guts to Jade.

Christ. I jab at a leaf of spinach, wondering how the hell I'm going to put the genie back in the bottle.

"What do you think if, right before the chorus, we change the progression to…" She names a series of chords.

It's a good tweak.

A *great* one, actually.

But something tells me that it's not just about the music right now.

Something tells me she sees right fucking through me.

It should be terrifying…

Only, as I look into those storm cloud gray eyes, that's not what I'm feeling.

"Jade?"

Her face falls. "You hate it?"

Music. *Just* music.

Thank God.

"No," I say. "I think it's perfect."

Like her.

CHAPTER SIXTEEN

Jade

AFTER DINNER, we settle back in the living room and pick up where we left off with "Midnight Snow." Despite having a nice breakfast together, I'm not sure what's going on with him because he's spent the day running hot and cold. One minute he's opening up about Colt and his found family. The next, he's surlier than ever, hunched over in the chair as I play the new chord progression.

"No?" I ask when he doesn't respond.

"It's fine," he says, in a weird tone of voice that tells me everything is anything *but* fine.

"I can tell when you don't like something," I say quietly. "Just say what it is. We're supposed to be a team here."

"It's not that I don't like it…I just feel like something is off."

"Like?"

"If I could show you, it would be easier, but I can't. So let me think, okay?" He snaps a little and I bite back an equally snippy response.

If he could show me *on the guitar*, it would be easier.

But he can't.

And my heart hurts for him all over again.

I lightly strum the chords leading into the chorus.

"That," he says, his face a little tight. "It's that progression right there. There's too much…*twang*."

Twang?

"Excuse me?" I frown. "What does that mean?"

"It's too country," he says, waving a hand. "It needs a little more rock and roll to it."

"Why?" I ask quietly. "What does that add to the song?"

"Everything."

I arch a brow. "You do know that we're writing this song for me, right?"

"I'm well aware." There's a note of annoyance in his voice that bugs me.

"If we were writing this for you, we'd need to make it more rock and roll. But we're not. In case you've forgotten, I'm a country-western singer. I don't play rock, so why would we write a rock song?"

"Because the songs *I* write sell," he says sharply. "And I have a few years of success under my belt. You know, like the song I wrote that won Song of the Year for you, in case *you've* forgotten."

"How could I forget? You bring it up as often as possible!" I glare at him.

"If you don't trust me to help your career then why the fuck are we here?" he demands.

I put down the guitar and slowly get to my feet. "Because you got your boxers in a bunch over what I said in that interview and somehow, convinced me this was a good idea. But I appear to have made a grave error."

"There's a reason your record company wants you to buy songs instead of using the ones you write yourself."

I open my mouth but can't think of a response.

And honestly, that hurts my feelings.

"What a rude thing to say," I respond quietly, trying to keep my feelings in check. "I think maybe I should go."

"Maybe you should." His blue eyes are as dark as... midnight.

As if he's truly angry.

And I'm not sure what I've done to evoke such a reaction.

I glance out at the four feet of snow we've gotten and realize I'm not going anywhere, except maybe to my room. "Mother Nature seems to have her own ideas about my leaving. But don't worry—I won't bother you with my silly little country songs anymore." I turn on my heel and stomp into my room, slamming the door behind me.

That was childish.

But I don't care.

He's such a jerk.

I can't believe I keep falling for his act the moment he says or does something sweet. I have to remember that the only person Royal Ewing cares about is himself.

Now I'm stuck in this damn cabin with him until the weather lets up, and even after it stops snowing, it could be a couple of days before we're shoveled out.

It's going to be a long few days.

I sink onto the bed, staring out at the bleak white landscape that's illuminated by the exterior lights. Earlier, it was so pretty and inspiring. Right now it's just a big blob of nothingness. Much like my heart.

I'm so empty inside, and I can't describe it.

Well, I can but I don't want to.

Because it's embarrassing to realize...I'm lonely.

I have fame, more money than I ever dreamed of, and am at the pinnacle of my success. And yet, I've never been more alone. I don't even have girlfriends. Not really. There are a couple of other country singers I'm friendly with. Lily Maxwell and Sandy Marin are great, and we hang out when we're in Nashville at the same time, but that's almost never.

They're both on tour, and Sandy just got married, so we don't see much of each other.

Aside from that, I've lost touch with everyone from high school, and though I have a couple of cousins, we don't know each other very well since we didn't grow up together.

So it's just me.

Puttering around a big, beautiful house in Tennessee with no one to share it with.

Living out of suitcases and hotel rooms on the road.

Spending time in a remote cabin with the world's biggest pain in my butt.

I don't even have anyone I can call to complain about him to.

I miss you, Grandma.

Thinking about her makes me even sadder.

I sink onto the bed and close my eyes, pulling the fleece throw over my lower half. I'm so mentally exhausted. And lonely. And sad. I have the elements of a great life, and when I'm making music, I don't care about anything else.

It's just the rest of the time that I get these waves of melancholy, but it's happening more often lately.

This new level of success I've suddenly attained has changed something. I can't quite put my finger on it but I'm less confident and much less content with the status quo, most of it to do with my personal life.

How is it that I don't have a single girlfriend I can call? I guess I could reach out to Sandy but she's on tour in Australia, and I don't even know what time it is over there.

I hate feeling sorry for myself, and I know this will pass once I get out on tour, but it's hard not to feel a little out of sorts with so many changes happening so quickly. With no one I can truly rely on to have my back.

It's frustrating and…

I must drift off because when I next open my eyes it's completely dark outside.

Crud.

How long did I sleep?

I reach for my phone and it's almost ten.

Great. I'll never get to sleep tonight.

A rumbling in my stomach lets me know that I'm hungry, which means it's time to face the music.

If nothing else, my bad mood is gone and I'm feeling a bit more philosophical. Being here with Royal has just been a stark reminder of how little else I have in my life besides music, and it's not his responsibility to pick up the slack for me.

We're stuck here for at least a few more days, so I need to go out there and apologize for storming off. I'm an adult and shouldn't have had a meltdown just because he hurt my feelings. I've been through a lot worse in this industry. He's just another difficult musician in a long line of them. He's not the first, and if he can write me another hit song or two, I won't need him or anyone else. I'll be able to write my own damn ticket.

I take a breath to steel my resolve, and my hand freezes on the doorknob.

There's music coming from the living room and I cock my head, listening.

Is someone playing guitar?

It can't be.

I quietly open the door and tiptoe down the hall.

Holy guacamole.

Royal is sitting on the chair by the fireplace, head bent over my acoustic guitar. The fingers of his left hand seem to be working the frets expertly but I can't see his right hand since he's turned away from me.

But God, what a sight.

Royal freakin' Ewing.

Basically in my living room, *playing guitar*.

It's soft, and there's no doubt he's not doing much with his right hand.

But he's doing it.

And my steely resolve goes right out the darn window.

His head is down, hair falling forward, so his face is shrouded, but I see the concentration. The struggle. The *frustration*.

And there's nothing I want more than to make that go away. To do something—anything really—to make it better.

I pad quietly into the room and before I realize what I'm doing, I'm standing behind him. His right hand is curved, pressed against the strings, and he's using his arm more than the hand to strum as best he can.

"Motherfu—" He starts to mutter more curses under his breath, and I bend over him.

"I've got you," I whisper, covering his right hand with mine and lightly squeezing.

I feel him stiffen but refuse to let him pull away.

"Just play. I can follow your lead." I drop my chin to his shoulder and move our hands in tandem. It's a simple motion, my hand guiding his on the strings.

But it works.

As if by magic, I feel the tension drain from his body. Feel him relax back against me. Feel him letting me in.

Letting me do this for him.

Neither of us say a word.

His eyes are closed now, and he's swaying slightly, practically becoming one with the guitar.

It's unlike anything I've ever experienced.

"Let's play it from the beginning," he says in a raspy voice. "Midnight Snow."

I already know the changes he's made are perfect.

"Yes." I stay right where I am, letting him guide the music while I move his hand.

And it's like we've done it a million times.

It's so easy to play together, sing together…do almost everything together.

Which is why it hurt my feelings so much when he made me feel like my contributions weren't valid.

Yet now we're playing it almost like we did before…and it's—

"Fucking perfect," he says, his voice thick with emotion.

"I know." I don't move, my hand still covering his, my front pressed close to his back.

"Thank you," he says softly.

"You're welcome."

He turns his head enough to look at me and the sizzle between us practically burns a hole into my soul.

"I really want to kiss you," he admits after a long moment.

"Then why don't you?"

CHAPTER SEVENTEEN

Royal

HER QUESTION SITS in the air between us.

She's pressed to my back, those lush tits making my cock go hard, her scent all around me, her hand covering mine somehow not feeling wrong.

The sensation isn't perfect.

The touch is dulled. The strings of the guitar as we played strange and unnatural.

But the song, sharing that with her…

It's like none of that mattered.

Matters.

"Royal?" she murmurs.

Carefully, I set the guitar to the side. Then reach behind me and tug her around to my front. She gasps as our legs tangle, her feet ending up in my lap.

"Sorry, I—"

The flames from the fireplace had gilded her skin, warmed her eyes, flushed her cheeks.

Or maybe that's the fire burning between us.

I pick up one bare foot, start gently massaging the sole before lifting it to my mouth.

Her eyes flare with shock. "What are you—?"

"You said to kiss you."

Her mouth drops open and I want to grin at how scandalized she looks right now. But, more, I want to make her feel good, want to make up for being such an asshole earlier.

I drop a kiss to the top of her foot and begin rubbing the other one, knowing I find the right spot when her eyes darken, hips shifting slightly on the oversized white furry rug. She melts and I coax her back, pressing my lips to her foot, her bare ankle. Her fabric covered knee. The bare sliver of skin on her abdomen that's exposed by her position.

"Even your belly button is cute," I say softly, chuckling as she inhales sharply and inching the fabric of her shirt higher, exposing more and more of that silken skin.

"Royal," she murmurs.

"More kissing?" I tease, following the pattern of freckles dotted along her stomach with my tongue.

"What are you doing?"

I still, lifting my head so I can meet her gaze, my fingers trailing over the skin I've bared, unable to *not* touch her. "Did you change your mind?"

"About what?" Her eyebrows are gathered into a tight frown, her eyes slightly glazed, as though she's struggling to make sense of my question.

"About the kissing."

Lips parting on a shuddering breath, she shakes her head. "I didn't change my mind."

"You want me to kiss you?"

A jerky nod.

I press my lips to her abdomen again. "Here?"

"No," she whispers. "I mean, yes, but no. Not *just* there."

I shift, dragging the material up, drawing it over her breasts, exposing her bra. And immediately, I want to forget about teasing, about making it up to her. I want to strip her naked, get my mouth on those tits, and fuck her hard and deep and fast.

"Lace?" I ask, holding tight to my control as I trace a finger along the scalloped edge of her bra.

"It's pretty," she murmurs, those tits bouncing because she's breathing rapidly now. "I like pretty things."

I grin at her. "Me too."

Up and down. Up and down. Up and down. I follow the curves along one breast and then the other.

"So," I say, "about the kissing…"

"Y-yes?"

"Here?" I ask, dragging my finger in, circling one taut bud of her nipple.

"Yes," she whispers. "And no."

"I like this game." I draw the shirt over her head, toss it to the side, then run my fingers along her throat.

"Here?"

A jerky nod, but I see the moment she fully commits to this. Her eyes heat, her lips part, and mischief creeps into her expression. "Yes. But also no."

I stroke a finger along her jaw, lift my brows in question.

"Yes." A beat. "No."

Her ear.

She smiles now. Shakes her head.

Same for her cheeks. Her forehead. Her nose.

"Hmm," I drawl. "Where am I forgetting?"

"Royal?"

"Yeah, Shortcake?"

But she doesn't respond—at least not with words. Instead, she threads her fingers through the hairs on my nape and draws my head down.

Our lips meet and before I can take over, she parts my mouth with her lips, slips her tongue into my mouth and lays a kiss on me that's so intense, I'm seeing stars. Maybe that's because all the blood in my body is currently in my dick.

Maybe it's because her kissing me brings me right back to that night.

Maybe it's because her lips on mine and her body beneath me and her hands holding me close feel right.

Not dulled. Not off.

Just...*right.*

"There," she says when we break apart, sucking in air. Her lips are swollen, her cheeks razor-burned, and her eyes are molten.

"Fucking beautiful," I growl and stop fucking around.

There are more places I want to kiss her. More places I *need* to get my mouth on.

But right now, I need to taste her again.

She moans when I drop my lips to hers, our tongues tangling, her leg wrapping around my waist, lining up our pelvises. She grinds against me, and I curse softly, knowing that my control is already unraveling.

Slow and deliberate.

Bringing her to orgasm after orgasm.

She deserves that and so much more.

"Royal?" she gasps when we break apart for air again.

"Hmm?" I ask, kissing one side of her mouth and then the other, her jaw, her earlobe. Along the column of her throat. Between her breasts.

I reach beneath her and undo her bra, drawing the straps down her arms and then I'm momentarily frozen, completely fixated on those gorgeous breasts that are now bared to me.

"Kiss me there?" she asks, innocent and not.

Sexy as fuck.

Unraveling more of my control.

More blood arrowing for my cock, eroding the last of my restraint, and I don't hesitate, don't dream of denying her.

I nip at the underside of one lush globe, roll the sensitive tip of the other between my thumb and forefinger, reveling in her gasps, her moans, the way the pink flush from her cheeks spreads down along her throat, across her chest.

Then I suck one nipple deep as I palm her tit, massaging and rolling and loving the way she says my name, rocks her hips.

I switch to her other breast, giving it equal treatment—or maybe getting lost in touching her, kissing her, *tasting* her.

At least until her hand weaves into my hair again and she tugs.

I release her nipple with a soft *pop*. "Yes?" I rasp.

Her breathing is unsteady, her words hoarse from her cries. "Royal?"

I drag my tongue along the curve of her breast. "Yeah, Shortcake?"

"Kiss me somewhere else?"

Soft presses of my mouth along her ribcage. "Here?"

A tug of my hair. "Lower."

Grinning, I nip at her skin, make my way down to her abdomen, to that adorable little belly button again. "Here?" I murmur against her skin.

"Uh—" She breaks off, hips bucking, head digging back into the rug. "Uh-uh."

"Hmm," I say, kissing my way over to her hip. "Where else could there possibly be to kiss you?"

She shivers as I trail my tongue in and down, not stopping until I reach the waistband of her pants.

"I got the feet, the ankles." I dip my tongue beneath the material. "Your lips and throat and those gorgeous breasts of yours."

Another shudder, her hips grinding against me. "Royal, *please*."

I almost give in.

Almost.

Because I want her so fucking badly that my cock feels like it's going to break in half.

But she likes this.

I see it in the heat in her eyes, the insistence in her words, the tight grip of her hand in my hair.

"Where else would you like my mouth, Shortcake?"

I expect her to continue to prevaricate, to tease and put off and hide behind the red cheeks and hint of shyness.

I *expect* to have to coax the words I want out of her, dragging them centimeter by centimeter.

Not that I'm complaining.

That's half the fucking fun—

Literally the *fucking* fun.

But I should have known better.

Jade is sweet and soft and beautiful, a gentle soul that is so easily trampled by the assholes in the world—and yes, I consider myself amongst that number.

She just doesn't have it in her to be difficult.

Not like me.

Not like—

Before the darkness sweeps over me, drags me out of this moment, she speaks again, her voice crystal clear and showing absolutely no hesitation.

"I want your mouth on my pussy, Royal," she says.

I gape at her, vision hazy, cock growing even harder.

But she's not done surprising the shit out of me.

Because then she says,

"And I want you to lick me until I come."

CHAPTER EIGHTEEN

Jade

I'VE NEVER BEEN SO brazen in my life.

But Royal isn't the type of man you can be too timid with. He's the kind of guy who'll eat you alive. Both physically and emotionally. If I'm going to be with him—in whatever capacity he'll allow—I have to show him I can give as good as I can get.

My body hums with the memory of his body on mine.

Around mine.

Inside of mine.

"Take them off," I say, lifting my hips so he can get my pants down. He takes my panties with them and then I'm naked. And he's still almost fully dressed.

I press my knees together.

"Your shirt," I rasp. "I like the view."

One side of his mouth tilts up in a wicked smile. "That so?"

He slowly, almost painfully, pulls it over his head.

"Now pants."

His eyes never leave mine as he drops them—along with his boxers.

Oh jiminy crickets, I love his penis.

I can't wait to feel it inside me again.

But first, his tongue.

And when he drops to his knees in front of me, my world is reduced to nothing but the expectation of what's to come—and the man before me.

The dark—but incredibly sensual—look in his eyes as he moves between my legs.

The way his unruly hair falls forward when he leans in, tickling the inside of my thigh.

The heat from his mouth as he presses a soft kiss there, then along the crease of my thigh, my pubic bone.

"You wet for me, Shortcake?"

My cheeks flush, but I nod, admit, "So wet."

"Hmm. I see that." He's staring down at the most intimate part of me, and yet I feel no embarrassment. This moment is everything I want it to be—and I know he feels the same just by the look on his face. He's normally so surly and closed off, but in this case, his face is the mirror of his soul. I know exactly what he's thinking, what he's feeling, just by how he looks at me.

With one finger, he gently traces a path between my legs, spreading the evidence of my desire around. I'm so turned on, my body completely in sync with his touch, it's hard to think. I like how it feels when he's touching me. Especially down there.

He leans in and drags his lips across my skin and then—oh sweet Jesus, that's good. His tongue is warm and wet against my swollen flesh, and I arch up to get more.

"Wait, baby…let me enjoy this—and you." His voice is gruff, as if taking his time is painful, and I sigh with a combination of excitement and frustration. I want more, but I want to slow everything down at the same time so this moment lasts longer.

"Oh!" My hips buck of their own volition when he sucks my clit into his mouth, but he presses me back down with the flat of his hand on my abdomen.

When he licks a trail down my slit, there's nothing I can do but go along for the ride. He's patient and skilled, as if he already knows everything I like. Because he does. His mouth, his lips—it's like every part of him is completely in tune with every part of me.

He dips a finger inside me, then two, moving them in tandem with his tongue.

"Oh, please!" I cry out, anxious for release. Doing it myself doesn't compare to how it feels when he makes me come, and my fingers find their way into his hair—something I've noticed I do a lot—tugging with urgency.

I feel his rumble of laughter against me, but he doesn't stop or pick up the pace—just continues his lazy, sensual assault on me. It feels amazing, but it's also sexier than anything I've ever done before, watching his dark head buried between my legs. And the sounds he's making—like I'm a delicious meal and he can't get enough—turn my insides to mush.

"Come on my tongue, baby," he orders, moving faster, deeper.

That's so hot, and I want to taste what he's tasting, but there's no time to ask because my orgasm is racing out of me like a freight train. I buck and writhe, making sounds I'm not sure I could ever replicate, and screaming his name.

"That's my beautiful girl," he rasps as I come down, lifting his head with a wicked gleam in his eyes.

Then, before I can process what's happening, he sheaths himself with a condom and slides his cock against my slick entrance.

"Royal." I whimper, grasping his hips, tugging him closer. "Touch me—kiss me!"

I lift my torso as he leans in and our mouths lock together greedily.

And when I taste myself on his tongue, the tangy flavor turns me on all over again.

"Please—do it now, Royal," I plead against his lips.

"Do what, baby? Can you say the word?"

I shake my head, biting my lip.

I've used the F word one time in my entire life. That was the day my grandmother taught me about speaking like a lady. And though I desperately want to whisper all the dirty words, I'm not sure I can.

"Please…" I reiterate. "*Please.*"

He pauses, the tip of his cock paused right at the edge of my entrance, and he smiles. "Okay, beautiful—we'll do it your way. *This time.*"

Then he slides in, one excruciating inch at a time, his eyes never leaving mine.

Oh. My. God.

Memories from the last time we made love come rushing back, and there's no mistaking the rush of liquid between my legs. I love how this feels, and I wiggle into a position that makes it more comfortable to accommodate his girth. He's huge and beautiful and hard and silky, and he's stretching me wide.

"You like that, Shortcake?" His eyes glitter with utter… *adoration.*

I can see it, feel it, know it. Whether it's real or just a moment of sexual perfection, I can't be sure, but right now—every part of him is mine. And I'm going to hang on to that as long as I can.

"Royal." I dig my nails down his back, pulling him closer. "Make love to me."

"We might have to save that for next time," he says through gritted teeth. "I'm hanging on by a thread right now. Fucking might be all I can give…"

"That's okay." I tilt my hips, taking him even deeper, and his eyes roll back in his head. "I'll be fast too."

"Fuck, baby, I can't—" He pulls back and slams back into me.

"Yes!"

"Can you take more?" he growls.

"Yes-yes-yes!"

There's no holding back or slowing down or taking our time.

This train is barreling down the track at full speed, my second orgasm imminent.

"Royal, I'm so close," I moan.

"You gonna cream all over my cock for me, Shortcake?"

"Yesss..." The word is drawn out as he pulls out again. Right to the tip.

"Look at me when you come," he growls. "Because I'm going to teach that sweet pussy who it belongs to."

This time I'm pretty sure it's *my* eyes that roll back in my head because—no matter what my brain is saying—my pussy most certainly wants to be his. Along with the rest of me.

"Royal!" He glides in and out a few times, watching my face, and then picks up speed.

"That's it, Jade...take it all..." He moves faster, pumping harder, hands on my breasts as he takes us over the edge.

"Yes!" A cry leaves my throat, even louder than the last, and I'm lost in a sea of endless pleasure. Endless need. Endless power.

That's the only word I can think of in the moment.

This is powerful, what we have.

And he knows it too because he collapses against me, boneless and drained, resting the side of his face on my shoulder.

"You are absolutely perfect," he whispers gruffly, enunciating each word carefully. "Every inch of you."

My heart stutters with pleasure—a different kind than what I just experienced.

How does he do this to me every time?

I don't want this feeling to end, but I also need things between us to be honest. I can't be with him any other way.

There can't be any games and we can't play with emotions this strong, no matter how much he may try to deny what's happening between us.

"I'm sorry about before," I whisper, winding my arms around him.

"Before?" He doesn't move, his breath warm against my skin.

"When we argued about the song, I stormed off. I shouldn't have behaved like—"

"I shouldn't have said what I said," he interrupts. "It was thoughtless. I was just…frustrated. But not with you."

"With yourself?" I gently stroke his hair, enjoying the feel of the silky strands between my fingers. Have I ever played with a guy's hair before? I don't think so. But I love touching Royal's.

"That's a pretty common state for me," he admits.

"You don't have to be frustrated when you're with me," I say. "I know who you are, no matter how hard you try to hide."

To my surprise, he very slowly lifts his head, searching my face in the semi-darkness.

The look we share leaves me with so much I want to say, but somehow, it doesn't seem necessary. There's something in the air that tells me everything I need to know.

"I believe you," is all he says before dropping his lips to mine.

CHAPTER NINETEEN

Royal

I THROW another log onto the fire, stoke the flames.

It's that midnight hour, the snow falling heavily outside, the world being slowly reduced to just Jade and me.

That would be so much simpler.

If it were just the two of us.

But it's not.

The music world is a brutal place, a cutthroat place.

And it's no longer my place.

But it's *her* place.

"My grandma used to say there was never anything quite as beautiful as a fire on a cold, snowy night."

She shivers slightly, and I move to the couch, snag the blanket from the back of it, and bring it over to her.

"Thanks," she whispers.

"Did you get a lot of snow in Tennessee?"

"Where the farm is? No." Her lips curve. "But some areas, sure, depending on what your definition of *a lot* is."

My lips twitch.

I seem to do that a lot around her.

She lifts the end of the blanket and jerks her chin behind her. "It's cold. Get in."

It's not cold, not really with the fire blazing and the heater going, but I can't bring myself to do anything other than crawl in behind her, wind my arm around her middle, drawing her back against my chest.

"Tell me about her," I order softly.

She shifts, her head tilting back, eyes coming to mine. "Who?"

"Your grandma," I say, but immediately regret making the request because the grief that slides into her expression is intense.

Damn.

"I didn't have any grandparents growing up," I find myself saying for no other reason than seeing her sad…hurts me. "But we kind of have one now."

Her eyebrows furrow. "What do you mean?"

"Aspen—you remember her?"

"Banks's wife. And Banks is the one I met who plays for the Vipers, right?"

A bolt of jealousy shoots through me. "You met Banks?"

Those storm cloud gray eyes study mine, a flicker of something I can't read crossing her face. "Yes," she says softly. "I met him and a few others briefly to sign autographs before I sang the national anthem the other day."

"Oh."

I brace, waiting for it, for her to say something to make me feel even more jealous, something my ex-wife, Amber, would have done, just to get a rise out of me.

Yes, I'm fully fucking aware that I have no right to feel possessive. I've done almost nothing except push Jade away.

And then find it impossible to truly let her go.

That doesn't stop the jealousy from snaking through my stomach, tangling up my insides.

She hung out with a bunch of hockey players.

Hockey players. I know what they were thinking about her, what they wanted to do to her, what—

"Banks mentioned his niece loved me and asked me to sign something." She covers my hand, the one that's resting on the gentle curve of her belly, with her own. "I signed, of course, along with a couple dozen other things for the employees and players who were there, but"—her lips twitch—"I think you're the uncle who's going to win, considering you made it so I actually got to hang out with Frankie."

The words take a second to penetrate, and when they do, I freeze, turning them over and over in my head.

She's not needling me.

In fact, she's comforting me.

And…that doesn't compute.

"What do you mean you kind of have a grandparent now?" she asks softly when I don't reply.

I blink then exhale slowly, clawing my way out of my head to focus on what she's asking. And truly, it's not a hard question to answer. "Aspen's next-door neighbor was this older lady named Mrs. X. She looked out for Aspen when things were really going rough for her, and now that Aspen and Banks are together, they're returning the favor. She's become an honorary member of the family."

"That's sweet," Jade murmurs.

"They're good people. And so is Mrs. X," I add, rolling to my back when she wriggles against me, as though searching for a more comfortable position. I draw her front against my chest, so she's lying on me instead of the rug, and smooth my good hand up and down her back. "Of course, she's also as much of a spitfire as Aspen is, so when those two get together…"

"Fireworks?"

"Sass and laughter and, yes, occasionally there are fireworks." A beat. "Though usually that only happens if someone insults Mrs. X's favorite actor."

"Who's that?"

"Patrick Stewart."

She mock gasps and then folds her arms on my chest, resting her chin on top of them. "Who would dare insult the great Patrick Stewart?"

I shrug, as much as I'm able in my position. "Someone who's dumb enough to miss out on Mrs. X's baking."

"She bakes?"

"And cooks. And meddles," I add because I like the way her eyes look when she smiles. "But mostly, she's a sweet, little old lady with a big heart whom we're lucky to know."

"My grandma was the same"—her eyes twinkle—"albeit without the Patrick Stewart obsession. She was a Denzel Washington fan—"

"Who isn't?" I say drolly.

She grins and keeps talking. "Though she did say Chris Hemsworth was quite pleasing to the eye before she passed."

I chuckle, tug at a lock of her hair, and tease, "Is that the kind of guy you like?"

She grins as she snags my hand. "No," she says. "I'm kind of partial to tall, dark, and broody myself."

"Don't, Shortcake." I draw my hand free, or try to.

She frowns, her fingers tightening around mine and I hate the sensation—dull, wrong, weak—the reminder—that my entire life imploded and I'm not good for this woman. "Don't what?"

I tug again, but don't say anything.

Can't say anything.

But she's smart, and I know the moment she gets it because of the way she changes her hold on my hand.

It doesn't go soft, like I would expect.

She tightens her grip and sits up slightly. "Because of your hand."

Normally, I'd shut this down, refuse to talk about it. *Normally.* I would pretend there isn't even an issue.

But those stormy gray eyes are on mine and I find that I… can't pretend to be okay.

"It feels wrong," I mutter.

"Wrong how?"

More questions that normally would be met with my fury.

But, just like I can't pretend to be okay, I also can't pretend to be pissed at her.

"You know about the accident—"

She nods. "They say that it wasn't your fault."

"I was speeding," I say, "so that's not completely right."

"Doesn't everyone speed in California?"

I wasn't expecting a joke and a laugh is torn out of me. "Yeah." I sigh. "I wasn't flying, but I was going ten over on a busy boulevard—not something I would have normally even thought twice about. But I was late to meet the guys at the studio and I was pushing it."

"And that's when it happened?"

I nod. "I was thinking about the song we were recording and how the chorus wasn't quite right and…I didn't expect the person to blow the red light."

She gasps.

"One second, I was closing in on the studio, and the next, I was…weightless as my car flew through the air." I sit up, draw her into my lap, the flash of memories too intense to just lie there.

As though she senses the adrenaline suddenly coursing through me, she doesn't fight me on the change in position.

"Then everything went black for who knows how long." I exhale. "I woke up with a concussion, a broken leg, and a mangled hand."

She tsks quietly and stares down at my hand, her fingers lightly tracing over the crisscross pattern of scars. They're mostly faded now, pale white and dull rather than red, lifted, and shiny. "That's how you got these?"

I resist the urge to pull my hand free. "Yeah. They thought I might lose it at first—or so my ex told me. I wasn't functioning on all cylinders then, too hopped up on drugs and in and out of surgery, so I don't remember those conversations. I just remember waking up a few days later in the hospital, after that fear had passed. Of course"—I chuckle darkly—"if I'd known I'd end up with this bullshit, I might have rather have it gone."

"Is it bad—?" She breaks off, starts again. "No," she says. "I know it's bad, bad enough that you can't play like you used to, but…what's the part that's actually stopping you from being able to?"

More shit I normally hate to talk about.

And yet, I just lay it all out there for her.

"Numbness, weakness, pain. Though the last one isn't so bad anymore. But I can't feel the strings well enough to play correctly, can't get my hand to do what it needs to. Fuck, just teaching Frankie 'Row, Row, Row Your Boat' is a challenge, let alone a Midnight Sun song or 'Forever in Rewind.'" I pull back now, flexing my fingers. "I can hear it—the melody, the chord progressions—but I can't *do* it."

She's quiet for a moment. "That must be incredibly frustrating."

"Yeah," I mutter. "I tried to get it back for a while, all the physical therapy, all the treatments, but after a year, the doctors told me it's probably as good as it's going to get."

"So, you took a break from music?"

I nod. "I can't play with the guys on tour and I didn't want to be the disabled millionaire guitar player with a sob story in the eyes of the world. It's bad enough the accident and then my divorce was everywhere."

"I'm really sorry," she whispers. "About your hand and the accident and the divorce. I can't imagine how hard it must have been."

"I was a real asshole for a while afterward."

"I mean," she says. "Isn't that, like, a typical reaction for someone with trauma?"

"Not according to Amber."

"Your ex?"

"She made it clear to me that she'd signed up to be married to a functioning rock star, not an asshole cripple with a hermit complex." I shrug.

Because, yeah, the words had hurt at the time.

But Amber was really good at hurting me.

Jade's reaction isn't so cavalier. She pushes out of my lap and bursts to her feet. "She said *what?*"

"You heard me right, Shortcake."

Her hands fist at her sides. A muscle in her jaw flexes. Bright red burns over her cheekbones. She opens her mouth, and I—never for a thousand years—would I have been able to predict the next words that come out of her mouth.

"Th-that...*strumpet!*"

CHAPTER TWENTY

Jade

ROYAL THROWS his head back and laughs.

Really laughs.

I don't think I've ever heard him laugh like this, and the sound is...wonderful. The look on his face, the pure joy in his eyes, catches me off-guard. He's already the hottest guy I've ever seen, but this side of him makes him a veritable heartbreaker. And Amber is a moron. What kind of woman abandons the man she supposedly loves after an accident like that?

"You're something, Shortcake." He brushes his mouth over mine, hovering, a smile still playing on his lips. "Thanks for making me laugh."

"Was what I said funny?" I wrinkle my nose.

"Honey, I'm almost positive I've never heard the word *strumpet* used in real life before."

I blush. "It was Grandma's favorite word for a woman she didn't think much of—and she wouldn't have liked Amber at all." I pause. "I don't either."

"Yeah, sometimes I still have a hard time believing I married her," he says thoughtfully.

"Did your friends like her?" I ask curiously. "Banks and Briar and the others?"

"Not particularly. They didn't dislike her, because in retrospect it seems like she was on her best behavior around them, but she didn't really spend much time with them either. I was touring then, and she was with me, so we didn't get together very often. Looking back, that probably should have been a huge red flag, but you know what they say about hindsight."

"Well, she was a fool," I say, putting my hand on the side of his face. "She didn't know what she had."

"Oh, I think she knew—she just didn't want it anymore."

"Like I said, she was a fool."

Our gazes lock, and the ever-present cloud of electricity seems to surround us.

His lips capture mine, his kisses soft and sensual, teasing, playful.

There might not be anything I enjoy more than the playful version of Royal.

Except maybe passionate, sexy Royal.

"I'm hungry," he says, rolling over. "You wore me out."

"*I* wore you out?" I counter, laughing. "I beg to differ."

"Are you hungry?" he asks pointedly.

I have to admit, my stomach could be down for a snack. "I could eat," I say, getting to my feet.

We pad into the kitchen together and I rummage in the fridge. "Cheese, crackers, fruit…impromptu charcuterie board?"

"Sounds good."

I pull out a handful of things that look good and begin arranging them on a platter I found on a top shelf. I hum as I work, slicing cheese and strawberries, adding a dollop of apricot jam, arranging the crackers, and placing a few slices of salami. I sprinkle a handful of grapes and turn to find Royal watching me with a smile.

"What?"

"Like I said, you're something," he says, stroking a finger along my jaw. "That looks amazing. Thank you."

"You're welcome."

"Do you spend a lot of time in the kitchen?"

"When I'm home, yes. Obviously, not when I'm touring or traveling, but I like to putter. That's when I get most of my song ideas."

"You were humming something just now."

"Midnight Snow," I admit then sigh contentedly. "It looks so pretty outside and reminds me of when I was little and we'd have snowball fights. Me, my parents, my grandparents…the whole thing was kind of magical."

"Yeah?" He follows my gaze and smiles. "When was the last time you had a snowball fight?"

"Years."

A slow, sexy smile. "I could change that."

I arch my brows. "I thought you were hungry?"

"I am, but a snowball fight at midnight with the most gorgeous woman I know sounds like a lot more fun."

I gaze out at the yard longingly.

It *does* sound like fun.

"I have to put on more clothes!" I say, practically running from the room.

And five minutes later we're outside, the floodlights on, a light snow still falling from the sky.

It's cold but I'm bundled up in sweats and gloves, a scarf, hat, and my winter coat. Royal is wearing sweats too, and a jacket, but doesn't seem nearly as concerned with the cold as I am.

"That isn't fair!" I tell him. "You're barely wearing anything—you have more mobility."

He rumbles out a laugh. "You're welcome to take off some layers."

And before I can react, he wings a snowball at me, catching

me right in the face. He didn't throw it hard, and the snow is still soft and fluffy, but I sputter indignantly anyway.

"*That* was not fair." I pack a bunch of snow together in my hands and give him the evil eye. "And now you're going to pay."

"Uh-huh." He laughs and dances out of the way.

I toss a few more snowballs in his direction, most of them woefully off-target, until one finally lands on the top of his head, sending clumps of snow down his face and onto his shoulders and chest.

"Now you're in trouble!" He growls playfully, scooping up a mountain of snow using both arms.

I shriek and make a run for it, tripping and landing face first in a snowbank.

"Jade!" I feel Royal behind me, lifting me out of my icy blanket. "You okay, Shortcake?"

He looks worried but I'm giggling, sputtering and shaking the flakes from my eyes. "I'm fine. Just a bit of a klutz."

He wraps his arms around me, pressing a kiss on the tip of my nose. "But a very *sexy* klutz."

I nestle closer and we stand there for a few seconds, staring up at the night sky. It's snowing harder now, probably an indication it's time to go back inside, but it's so pretty I can't make myself move.

"It's midnight," he whispers, glancing at his watch.

"And snowing," I say, tilting up my face expectantly.

He doesn't disappoint.

His lips find mine with a sweetness I've never felt from anyone.

How is this guy real?

And how am I supposed to go back to reality when this snow-filled fantasy is over?

THE SNOW FINALLY STOPS FALLING, plows come to clear the roads, and by day six, it's time to go. I woke up nestled in Royal's arms again this morning, we had breakfast together, made love in the shower, and now we're on our way to the airport.

I don't know where the time went.

Or what's going to happen next.

And I'm a little afraid to ask.

But I have to.

I'm going home to Nashville—for the first time in over a month—and he's heading to L.A. Our paths likely won't cross again unless we make plans.

"Royal?" Our fingers are twined between us in the car driving me to the airport.

"Yeah, babe?"

"Am I going to see you again?"

He's quiet for what feels like a long time.

So much so my heart starts to sink.

I was prepared for disappointment—but not how bad it actually feels.

"Is that what you want?" he asks after long seconds ticked by. "I'm not good for you, Jade. I'm not good for anyone."

"Says who?" I shake my head. "You don't scare me, Royal Ewing."

"But I should." He turns his head, his eyes searching mine. "I'm broken. Scarred. And surly as fuck. Why would you even want this?"

"You're also handsome and talented and strong. Most people would have given up after what you went through—but you're still here, writing music, supporting your friends, and being the world's best uncle to a little girl who worships the ground you walk on. Children *know* when someone is inherently bad. So Frankie wouldn't love you the way she does if you were."

Something akin to gratitude flickers behind his eyes, and

then he does what he always seems to do when he wants to avoid an emotional conversation—

He kisses me.

And I let him because…well, because I like it. Because I know it's not a sexual deflection so much as a way for him to show me what he's not always able to articulate.

Feelings are hard for Royal.

I discovered that pretty quickly, so now I have a better handle on what he needs from me.

Assuming he wants to see me again.

We've arrived at the airport and the car is slowing down, which means I need an answer, one way or the other. It will hurt—a lot—if he doesn't want to see me again, but now that I know what he's been through, I'm not going to add to the stress in his life.

"I have to go," I whisper, breaking the kiss.

"I know." He presses his lips to my forehead, the tip of my nose, the underside of my jaw.

"Royal, if you don't want to see me again, please just be honest. I don't like being ghosted. It hurts too much and it's disrespectful. We're adults. If our weekend was just another one-off—"

"No. Stop." He puts a gentle finger on my lips. "That's not what it was. We both know that. I just don't want to hurt you again. I don't know that I'm…boyfriend material. Not anymore."

"Shouldn't that be for me to decide?"

"I'm not always nice."

"We'll work on it."

His lips twitch, as if he's fighting a smile.

"You're amazing, you know that?"

"Ms. Cantrell?" John cracks open the door. "Are you ready?"

"I have to go," I whisper to Royal.

He presses his lips to mine. Hard.

There's a promise in that kiss.

I feel it.

I'm not sure what the promise is, but it's there.

"Call me when you get home and we'll figure something out," he says in a gruff voice. "That okay?"

"Yes." Relief and happiness wash over me. "It's more than okay."

It's not over.

The trip is over, but *we* aren't over.

There's no time to celebrate, though. John is waiting patiently, so I start to get out of the car. Only to find myself halting when Royal gently tugs the back of my jacket.

"Jade?"

"Yes?" I look over my shoulder at him.

His blue eyes burn into mine. "'Midnight Snow' is going to be your next big hit."

"Our next big hit," I correct firmly.

One side of his mouth quirks up. "*Our* next big hit."

CHAPTER TWENTY-ONE

Royal

THE MUSIC BLASTS, and the bar is full.

And every time I walk through the doors to The Sapphire Room, I can't help but think that Colt would love it here.

That's the point, though, isn't it?

To create a place he would have fucking *loved.*

Well, mission accomplished.

I sit in the back, at the table with the small brass sign engraved with *Reserved for Colt.* It's always kept empty unless one of us is here.

Tonight it's full of Gamebreakers.

Banks because the Vipers don't have a game and Aspen's working—and right now, where Aspen is, is where Banks is.

Or I guess it's been that way from the moment he first fell for her.

Dash because he's in town and not working for once.

Atlas because he's the most hands on of all of us with the club. His business acumen and control freak ways make him the perfect candidate for being in charge of the day-to-day operations.

And me.

I'm rarely at the club unless the guys—or Briar—make me, and yeah, that problem gives even more credence to what I was telling Jade before we flew out this morning.

I'm no good for her.

I'm no good for *anyone*.

I can't even bring myself to spend time with my friends, with my *family*. It's only the creeping silence in my house—no Jade in the kitchen, humming as she cooks; no Jade sputtering, snow melting on her eyelashes; no Jade curled up beside me in bed, her lush little body pressed to mine; no Jade—

No *Jade*.

She texted me to let me know she arrived safely in Nashville—a text I stayed pathetically glued to my cell, waiting for it to come in.

And I'd replied I was glad she safely made it.

And…

That was it.

She's going back to her life. I'm back in mine.

Except, I promised that we'll figure something out.

I just…

Have no fucking clue what that means, no fucking clue what I can give her, no fucking clue what I'm *doing*.

And I couldn't sit at home in my silent, empty house one more night.

So, when Banks texted the group chat and said he was coming to The Sapphire Room tonight and the guys chimed in that they were available and would join him—with the exception of Briar (who's one of us guys, for all intents and purposes), and who's having a self-care Saturday (whatever the fuck that means) with Frankie—I decided to join the guys.

Better sitting around brooding here than at home.

Dash jabs his elbow into my side, and I glare at him. "What?"

He jerks his chin toward Banks—who's drinking in the sight

of Aspen behind the bar like she's the only drop of water in the Sahara Desert. "Whipped."

"Aren't we a little old to be giving each other shit about women?" I grumble.

Atlas picks up his Gamebreaker and reclines back against the black leather of the booth. "Nah. We're never too old to give each other shit about anything—but most especially women."

I roll my eyes.

Dash grins.

Banks barely spares us a scowl. "Fuck off. Aspen hasn't been feeling well."

We all sit up a little straighter.

"What do you mean?" Atlas asks brusquely. "She was fine at Christmas."

"She's not feeling well," Banks semi-repeats. "She's puking all the time, tired, and she passed out today."

Atlas sets his drink on the table with a *thunk,* sending liquid sloshing over the rim. "What the actual fuck, Banksy?" he snaps. "There is no way she should be here tonight—"

"Oh believe me," Banks mutters, and I realize that he's drinking water. "I know."

So totally whipped.

And worried.

And—

"I tried to tell her to stay home"—he tosses up his hands—"but would she listen to me? Of course fucking not."

Dash and my gazes connect and we exchange a knowing wince. As much as we might like to think that we could control the women in our life—cough *Briar*—they've more than often decided to have their own minds.

Which is a thought I'm going to keep to myself—secure and well away from the women in my life.

But, seriously, case in point?

Briar and her stubborn independence.

And Frankie, her little mini-me.

And—I slant my eyes to the bar, where a certain brunette spitfire is dutifully serving customers, despite the dark circles under her eyes and the pale skin—Aspen.

And…

Jade.

She's sweet, kind, and possesses a rather impressive stubborn streak.

I'm not afraid of you, Royal Ewing.

Well, she should be.

"I'll fire her," Atlas says, his overprotectiveness meaning that he's fully prepared to go with the nuclear option. "In fact"—he drops his palms to the table, starts to push up to his feet—"I'll tell her right now."

That has Banks snapping out of it, fisting the back of Atlas's suit and tugging him back down into the booth. "No, you fucking won't," he snaps. "Aspen loves this place and is just starting to get comfortable in her position—" He rips his eyes from the woman he loves and glares at Atlas then all of us in turn. "No one is going to jeopardize that."

"Got it, Banksy," Dash mutters.

I lift my hands, palms out, in surrender.

Atlas takes the longest to cave—he is protective of women in general, but most especially of women who've been through the ringer (like Briar, and *definitely* like Aspen)—but he eventually nods and grumbles. "Fine. I won't fire her." A beat. "Yet."

I want to laugh, but I'm smart enough to keep my mouth shut.

Which I mostly do by finishing off the rest of my drink—and then ordering another from the bar.

Aspen serves me with an edgy smile. "Another Game-breaker?"

"You good?" I ask quietly.

"If Banks is asking," she says tartly, "then I'm fucking perfect, and he can stop freaking out."

Yikes.

"And if it's me?"

She winces. Then sighs, closes her eyes for a second. "Sorry. I'm good. I'm pregnant and sick all the time and I've taken more naps in the last month than I've had in a lifetime, but I'm…"

"Good?" I finish.

She nods.

"Aspen?" I ask as she turns to help another customer.

"Yeah?" she asks, that edginess drifting back in.

"You might be a little better if you let Banks take care of you." I lift my hand, holding my thumb and pointer finger apart by maybe a centimeter. "Just a smidge," I add and wink at her. "Because *he'll* definitely feel better."

I brace for fire (there's a reason Banks calls this woman spitfire), but her face softens and her mouth hitches. "You're smart, Royal Ewing," she says, leaning over the bar and pressing a kiss to my cheek. "Tell him I'll finish this rush and then he can take me home, will ya?"

Saluting, I turn back for the guys.

"What did you say to her?" Banks demands.

"Relax," I mutter. "We were shooting the shit, but she did ask me to tell you…" I relay the news about the rush and going home and watch as the tension in both Banks and Atlas relaxes.

"What's that about giving each other shit about women?" I ask pointedly.

"Speaking of that…" Dash trails off and I lift my brows at him in question. "...are we going to talk about the hickey on your neck?"

He jerks at the collar of my shirt.

I freeze.

What the actual fuck?

Then I bat his hands away. "Get fucked," I snap.

But it's too late. Banks leans in and tugs my shirt down. "It *is* a fucking hickey. What?" he asks, and it's the first time I've seen him joke all night (and of course, it's at my fucking expense). "Are we in high school again?"

"Yeah," I grind out, "like a girl would touch you in high school. Weren't you a virgin until college?"

"Nice try"—he grins—"Becky Connor. Eleventh grade."

"Congrats," I say dryly and drain my glass, consider another. Unfortunately, I drove here so I can't make this conversation go away by getting drunk.

"Wait," Dash says. "Weren't you with Jade Cantrell over the weekend?"

I open my mouth.

"Yup," Atlas says before I can lie. "Spending the weekend *songwriting*."

"So did *that*"—he grins and nods at my neck—"happen between writing the chorus and the second verse?" Dash asks.

Atlas snorts.

Banks busts up.

"Fuck off," I growl.

"Ah, man," Dash says, clapping me on the shoulder. "Relax. We're just happy you fucked someone other than a harpy or a groupie."

My temple starts throbbing.

But thankfully the guys pick up that I'm at the end of my rope—or that I'm ready to flip the table and get the fuck out of here—because they change the subject. Atlas discusses his latest business ventures, along with the extra travel that will come with it. Dash mentions he picked up doing a security rework for a big time Hollywood actor with a stalker problem. And Banks talks about hockey—and how things have finally leveled out for him.

I don't share about getting snowed in with Jade, about setting the sheets on fire, about the snowball fight, and all the other things, the feelings, the promises. Those are for me—for us—only.

But I do tell them about working with her.

"She's fucking smart, man," I say. "And talented. She can hear the music before it's even played and has the singing chops to back up what's running through her mind." I shake my head. "I've never written so many songs or done it so easily."

"Impressive," Atlas says.

"Yeah." I pick up my glass, drain the dredges as silence falls between us.

Thankfully, they don't give me shit for once.

Or maybe that's because Aspen is heading our way, clearly having wrapped up what she needed to wrap up.

Banks jumps to his feet, starts for her, then stops. "I almost forgot. I got ice time next Tuesday. You guys in for some old school Gamebreaker action?"

"I'm in," Atlas says. "My plane out isn't till Thursday."

"Righteous," Dash says, extending his fist for Atlas and then Banks to bump. "You both know I'm in."

Three sets of eyes come to mine.

I shrug, pushing past the uneasiness that flicks the back of my psyche. "I'm in too."

Now three sets of eye*brows* shoot nearly to their hairlines.

"You're *in?"* Banks asks.

I glare at him. "That's what I said, isn't it?"

Banks looks at Atlas, who shrugs. "That *is* what he said."

"Christ," I mutter, that throb in my temple growing.

"Fuck, man." Dash claps me on the shoulder again, so hard that my teeth click together— which is probably for the best because it stifles what I would say in response to his next words.

"You need to marry this one."

CHAPTER TWENTY-TWO

Jade

I'VE BEEN on the phone for nearly three hours.

Three long, miserable, frustrating, and unproductive hours.

It's maddening, how stubborn my management company is being. They're so far up the record company's behinds, they must be seeing brown.

And I'm furious.

They're pushing back hard against firing Farrah, so much so that they've refused to do it. She didn't realize how much the personal questions would bother me. Plus, since I'm such a big star she assumed I'm used to it. She's apologized at least a hundred times, and both she and my management company have practically filled my house with flowers and baskets of goodies.

I'm physically and mentally exhausted because it feels like no one has my back.

Not a single person in my life supports what I want to do. How I want to run my career. What I expect from the people who work for me.

It's my own fault because I've been too easy going for too

long. In the beginning, I trusted the record label and my manager to do what's best. Now that I know better—and they see that their money train might be leaving the station without them—they're trying to control me.

Not only that, the news that I've decided to let Royal produce my next album has them freaking out.

"…Jade, honey, I know he wrote a huge hit for you, but is this really the guy you want hitching his star to yours?" My manager, Norma, has asked me this three times already.

"Yes, as a matter of fact, I do," I reply, also for the third time.

"Have you done the research?" Farrah asks.

Not that I give a hoot what she thinks.

"Look at this." She sends me the link to an article.

Rock superstar Royal Ewing in physical altercation with wife.

Amber.

That harlot.

"The woman who told him she had no interest in staying married to a guy who couldn't play guitar anymore?" I snort. "I probably would have hit her too." He didn't hit her, though. I know this story because he told me every detail.

"Sweetie, we're just worried about your reputation," Farrah says in a sickeningly sweet voice.

"My name," I say icily, "is *Ms. Cantrell*. Unless and until I tell you otherwise. And where was all this concern about my reputation when Liza was asking me wholly inappropriate questions?"

"Oh, Jade." Norma sounds disappointed in me. "We've already acknowledged that Farrah made a mistake. One she'll never make again."

"Never, ever," Farrah promises.

This whole thing is so ridiculous—we've been going round and round for hours—I almost laugh at the absurdity.

"You know, the guy who produced one of Garth's early albums—" Norma begins.

"No." I say it flatly and lean back in my chair. We're on a video chat, so they can see me, and I'm sure there's no doubt how annoyed I am. "I'm not going old school. That's not my style. I love Garth, but his music isn't my music."

"Well, what is your music?" Farrah asks. "That way we can spin it correctly."

"There's no spin!" I say in frustration. "It's just music. Royal and I wrote at least four songs for the new album, and I wish you would trust that I know what I'm doing. You handle the tours and merch and advertising and marketing. I handle the music. Right?"

There's a long silence that makes me want to grit my teeth. Possibly start throwing things.

"Your music alone didn't get you where you are," Norma says. "There are a thousand talented, attractive singer-songwriters in Nashville. And no one knows their names. You got where you are because of us. Because we showed you how to do it and got the right songs in front of the right people."

A touch of unease snakes its way through my system, nearly taking the wind from my sails.

Royal told me to stand up for myself. He assured me I have the strength and the power to run my career the way I want to. But it doesn't feel like it.

These people—whether I like them or not—have been instrumental in getting me to the top. The fact that I want to drop them now that I'm there feels wrong. No matter how uncomfortable they make me.

I know what I want to do but making it happen suddenly feels impossible.

I wish Royal was here.

Figuratively—or literally—holding my hand and reminding me that I can do this.

That I can do *anything*.

I've never been the type of woman who needs a man's help to navigate life, but the music business is a completely separate—and much more scary—entity.

Fortunately, I don't have time to argue anymore.

"I'm sorry, guys," I say finally. "Rico Galagos is coming over for lunch, so I have to go. We can pick this up again on Monday. Thank you." With that, I disconnect. It feels a little bit rude but I don't care. Rico really is on his way, he texted that he's ten minutes out, and I'm looking forward to seeing him.

He's someone I've always been able to count on, so maybe he'll have a different perspective for me. I'd been both surprised and excited when he'd mentioned he was going to be in Nashville because this isn't really his scene. I didn't hesitate to invite him over for lunch, though.

"Baby girl, you look amazing!" Rico whistles as he comes through the door. He's never been to my house in Nashville before, and we do a little tour.

"I tried to update and modernize without losing the charm," I explain when we get to my incredibly contemporary primary bathroom.

"Look, ain't nobody got time for avocado green appliances or ugly showers," he says firmly. "You've got lots of charm while still immersing yourself in luxury."

"That's what I think too."

We make our way back to the kitchen, and I start pulling out the quiche I made, along with salad, fruit, and pomegranate lemonade.

"Do you cook?" he asks, wide-eyed.

"Of course." I cock my head. "What self-respecting Southern girl doesn't cook?"

He grimaces. "None that I know. But I don't know that many."

We chuckle together.

Sitting at the island, we eat and catch up, and I tell him what happened with Farrah.

He wrinkles his nose. "She's always been a little entitled, you know? Like her clients should be grateful for her presence in their life."

"I'm not at all grateful. Honestly, she hasn't done anything for me. I had someone else before the record company forced her on me. Mostly, she annoys me."

"There's a game to be played, though, and you could use this to your benefit."

"What do you mean?"

"Well, when you want something next time, something that's bigger than this pissing contest you have going with Farrah—you say, well, when I wanted Farrah gone, I towed the company line. This time, I want you to take a hit for me. Or whatever."

He has an interesting point.

And maybe I can use that to get Royal to produce my album.

"I want you to listen to something," I tell him excitedly, reaching for my phone. Royal and I made better recordings, but I love the ones on my phone because they're both intimate and raw, with a little bit of Royal's grittiness. Something I've started to love.

I play him "Midnight Snow," practically bouncing in my seat as I wait for his reaction.

"Damn, girlfriend." He nods with a big smile. "That's got the makings of a hit. Will you send me a copy? I'd love to hear it in my studio."

I do a happy little wiggle as I scroll through my voice memos so I can send him the right recording. If Rico likes it…eek! Then it's *really* good. "Of course." I tap out the message, attach the file, and listen to the little whoosh as it's sent off through cyberspace. "Done!"

"Thanks, babe." He squeezes my hand. "I can't wait to see where this takes you."

"I know. Me too." I'm probably grinning a little too much, but I can't help it.

"Is it for the next album?"

I nod.

"Who are you gonna get to produce it?" There's a gleam in his eyes and out of nowhere, it hits me what today was all about.

Crud.

He's never come to visit before because he didn't need anything.

Now he does.

After my recent success, he's the next one jumping on the money train—he wants to produce the next album.

Darn.

"Royal Ewing is going to produce," I say quietly. "We work well together. We wrote 'Midnight Snow' in a couple of hours." That's a bit of an exaggeration, but he doesn't need to know about all the kissing and touching and making out that went on in between making music.

"I see." He puts his fork down and meets my gaze steadily. "So…are you planning to replace *everyone* who got you where you are?"

Guilt slices through me.

"Rico, no. That's not it at all. Remember, you turned me down when I asked you to work on my second album, because you were doing more hip hop—I didn't think you *wanted* to do country at all anymore."

"But you could have asked." His dark eyes are sad.

And I really hate that it's because of me.

"I'm…*sorry*. Truly. You never said anything."

"I didn't think I had to." He wipes his mouth and stands up. "And you already asked Royal, didn't you?"

"Well, yes." Not officially, but we discussed it. Again, not something I plan to share because this is so awkward already.

I nervously chew the inside of my cheek.

"Please don't go," I say quietly. "Maybe you can produce one of the songs and collaborate on—"

"Give me a break. That's the equivalent of a pity fuck," he says, shaking his head. "This isn't my first rodeo, Jade. And I guess you're going to learn the hard way about not stepping on people on your way to the top. They're the same people you have to pass on your way back down."

My mouth opens but nothing comes out.

I'm too shocked to formulate a response.

"I think you should go." That's all I manage to choke out once I find my voice.

"When Royal Ewing chews you up and spits you out, don't come crawling back to me," he says as he heads for the door.

He closes it softly behind him and all I can do is stare.

What in the world just happened?

Why would he talk to me this way?

I thought we were friends.

Apparently, I was wrong.

Standing there in my foyer, the surge of loneliness that hits me is so strong, I almost can't breathe. And then, because I'm just so tired of everything, I burst into tears.

CHAPTER TWENTY-THREE

Royal

"PASS, PASS!" I look up, see Banks streaking down the ice, and instinct takes over.

I flick the puck toward him, sending it across the rink just before Atlas slashes me hard across the hands.

Fucker.

The sting slides up both of my palms and I have to fight to keep hold of my stick.

Luckily, they took pity on the man with the bum hand and put me on the team with Banks and a few of his former and current teammates. Atlas, Dash, and the others are mostly old-timers, one current pro player, and a mechanic named Briggs, who has a surprisingly wicked slap shot.

Banks scoops the shitty pass up and cuts in toward the net.

God, he's smooth.

And we're all playing nice—

All, except Atlas, who struggles to turn off his competitive edge, no matter the occasion.

He starts chasing Banks down, his expression intent (and maybe a little murderous).

Luckily, Banks gets the shot off—not his full ripper, but a nicely placed wrist shot that the goalie has to scramble to catch. He covers it…

Right as Atlas reaches Banks, giving him a light crosscheck for his trouble.

And *light* sends Banks to his ass.

"Rude," Banks mutters, getting up…and doing so with his stick between Atlas's legs…

Atlas goes down like a ton of bricks.

Dash skids to a halt beside me, digging in his skate blade at precisely the right angle to shower Atlas with snow.

Our billionaire friend sputters indignantly and—fuck me—my heart squeezes when I remember Jade doing the same thing, albeit much more daintily.

And prettily.

"Asshole," Atlas snaps, reaching out and wrapping an arm around Dash's leg, sending him toppling to the ice to do some sputtering of his own.

I freeze.

Then bust up laughing, so hard that I let my guard down—

"Shit!"

I fall forward—okay, I'm *shoved* forward—landing hard on the ice with a grunt…

And Banks on my back.

"Fucker!" I growl, reaching for him.

We grapple for a few moments, but then the grappling turns into laughter and shit talking, and pretty soon we're all back on our feet and focused on the game.

We skate until my lungs feel like they're going to explode and my legs shake so much I'm pretty certain I won't be able to walk tomorrow. But by the time we call for a break and suck down water on the bench, I'm energized in a way I haven't been in years.

Then we jump right back out there.

And I'm glad.

Because I've missed this—the strength and speed, camaraderie and shit talk, the high that comes when I connect a pass or score a goal—and considering it's a pickup game and there isn't a whole lot of defense being played, I score a handful. But, more than that, I miss the time in my life when shit was simpler.

It was a small gig and eking out a win in a college game.

It was mixing our own Gamebreakers and getting drunk as fuck in a shared on-campus apartment.

It wasn't getting random news stories written about me or hearing about the latest drama I'm creating in a TikTok video.

It wasn't walking outside and having someone pepper me with questions to try to get a rise out of me.

And it wasn't…

Jade.

That pit in my stomach that had been opening up, threatening to consume me, to send me spiraling with all the things I wanted and how they didn't end up being as great as I expected them to be—losing Colt; the guys and I trying to keep it together for Briar and Frankie; the conflict in the band as I struggled to balance that and create art *and* keep to the schedule the record company demanded of us; the politics between agents and media and producers; the accident and Amber leaving; the news and recovery afterward—all of that freezes with just four little letters.

Jade.

"Heads up!" Banks calls, and I snap out of my head enough to see Atlas tearing toward me with the single-minded focus that is so totally Atlas.

So much for a friendly game.

My lips twitch, but I manage to side-step the charging Atlas and get the pass off.

And then I'm not in my head.

It's just the game—the calls from my teammates, the cool

rush of air against the overheated skin, the sting of the passes hitting my stick blade. My hand isn't perfect, but it's much better than when I'm trying to play my guitar. Gross motor versus fine motor, and really the passing and shooting is all about wrist and elbow movement and weight transfer, not being able to strum guitar strings in rapid succession.

I brace for Atlas when he circles back, shove him off, and I'm glad that he's not actually trying to take me out when he lets me.

"Easy, fucker," I tell him.

He just grins, like he's having the time of his life.

And it's such a shocking change from his normal stoic self that I find myself standing still, mouth agape.

At least until Banks skates by and smacks me on the ass with his stick. "Move it, Royal."

I scowl at him, but it's just for show, and then I'm moving again.

We play until the Zamboni doors open and they kick us off the ice.

But I'm still riding the high as we walk down the hall to the locker room and start getting undressed.

I'm just tossing my skates into my bag when Banks shoves his cell into my face. "Look," he orders, hitting the button to start the video someone took.

I grin as I watch me pass him the puck on the screen. Watch as he dips and dances, using some of his lightning speed to streak up the side of the ice. But I'm right behind him, my stick on the ice, waiting because I know—

And yup, there it is.

He chips the pass over to me…and because the man's got the goods, it settles right on the flat of my blade, perfectly on target.

All I have to do is flick my stick and—

"Nice fucking shot," Banks says, bumping his shoulder against mine.

I grunt at the compliment. "Send that to me, would ya?"

He looks at me sideways—probably because we don't take

this kind of stuff seriously, and I've never asked him to send me a video before, not unless it was of Frankie being adorable, that is. But he doesn't comment, just texts it over to me.

I pull out my phone, take an obscenely long time trying to find the right words to accompany it, then just decide on—

ROYAL: Remember that whole hockey thing?

She takes what feels like an equally obscenely long time to respond, but in actuality, it can't be very long since I've just begun to remove my shin guards when I feel my phone buzz from next to me.

JADE: I sure do.

My lips twitch and my fingers move rapidly on the screen.

ROYAL: Well, look at what I did today.

ROYAL: And I hope you'll be suitably impressed.

ROYAL: *video*

Another long moment of anxious waiting—my jersey hitting my bag, along with my shoulder and elbow pads.

JADE: I am very impressed.

ROYAL: What other things about me impress you?

I add a smirk emoji as I watch the "..." dance, indicating her typing out a text.

"Really?" Banks asks dryly. "You think that shit will work?"

"Shut the fuck up," I snap, shoving down my hockey pants and tossing them with the rest of my equipment into my bag.

She texts me back after I tug off my jock—because my dick and hockey pucks don't mix. Not to mention that the assholes I was playing with would totally cup check me given the opportunity.

But her message has me frowning.

JADE: I really AM impressed. And it's really cool of you to share that after all you told me about hockey and the guys, but I'm kind of dealing with a situation right now. Can we talk later?

ROYAL: Are you okay?

JADE: I'm fine. I've got it covered. I'll fill you in later.

ROYAL: Okay. Talk soon.

My scowl is real this time as I stare at the screen, trying to see through the words to figure out what the real problem is.

Her publicist? The record company? Something else?

"What is it?" Banks lips twitch. "Your bad pickup lines?"

I shove him back. "Fuck off, yeah?" Then I go back to staring at the screen.

Banks tilts his head to the side. "Damn," he murmurs. "You're serious?"

I shoot him a look and ask dryly, "What do you think?"

"And you're worried?"

Every instinct inside me is screaming at me to shut the fuck up and avoid this conversation.

Instead, the word is torn out of me. "Yeah."

"Let me see?"

I grit my teeth, but pass over my cell, ignoring the bolt of pain that shoots through my jaw as I wait for him to read the messages.

"Well," he says, passing it back to me.

"Well what?" I snap.

"It's settled."

What the fuck?

I glare at him. "*What's* settled?"

"She needs you." He shrugs. "So you're gonna go to her."

CHAPTER TWENTY-FOUR

Jade

WHEN ROYAL ASKED me for my address because he wanted to send me something, I was expecting a mountain of flowers to arrive. What I didn't anticipate was him standing there on my front porch delivering them personally.

"Royal?" I gape at him for a moment and then launch myself into his arms.

"Hey, baby." He hugs me awkwardly since he's holding the flowers with his good hand, but it doesn't matter. Our mouths move together hungrily, as if it's been a lot more than a week since we last touched, and I finally tug him inside.

"What are you doing here?" I demand, taking the flowers from him.

"I got the vibe you need me," he says quietly, meeting my gaze.

My heart stutters with happiness, and tears inexplicably prick my eyelids.

I don't know how, but he knew something was wrong.

And he just showed up.

"How did you know?" It seems important for some reason.

"Everything you weren't saying told me something was up. And based on your reaction just now, I'm guessing I was right."

For someone who says he isn't good for me, I'm not getting that vibe at all.

I can't remember the last time someone showed up for me without me asking. At least, someone who wasn't after something.

"You have no idea." Embarrassed by how emotional I'm feeling, I head for the kitchen to find a vase and he pads behind me. "But let's get settled first. I'll show you around once I put these in water."

"This is beautiful," he says a couple of minutes later as we walk through my living room. "I love the fireplace."

"It used to be wood burning, but I had them make it gas. I don't have the time or energy to build fires. My grandfather made the mantel, though. I'll never change it."

"It's gorgeous," he says. "And the windows…"

I have floor-to-ceiling windows on one wall, giving me a ton of light and an even better view.

"Yeah, that's one of my favorite things about the house."

I show him around, and somehow, we end up in the bedroom. I sink onto the edge of the bed and rub my temples.

"I'm really glad you're here," I whisper, suddenly emotional again.

"Why didn't you tell me something was going on?" he asks, sitting beside me and taking one of my hands in his.

"Because it's my problem…Grandma taught me not to rely on anyone because people inevitably let you down. And she's never been more right."

"You consider me one of the people who's going to let you down?"

"I don't know," I admit. "I don't want to think that, but it hasn't been that long, and you've…made it clear that you're not into relationships."

"I also said we were going to figure it out."

"Yes, but we haven't had any conversations about that since the cabin."

"Well, I'm here now and I'm not going anywhere." He strokes his fingers over my cheek. "Talk to me, Jade. What's been happening?"

"So much." I don't even know where to start, but the situation with Farrah feels easiest. I catch him up on that, tell him what happened on our conference call, and then segue into Rico's visit.

"I thought you and Rico were close?" he asks, interrupting me.

"I thought so too. Until I told him that I wanted *you* to produce the next album."

His eyes widen. "Wait—is that why he came to visit? To pitch his production services?"

"Apparently."

"Motherfucker." He shakes his head. "What a fucking douche."

"You don't seem surprised."

"Honey, I told you about these types of things—this is how it goes. That's why you need a strong, solid team around you. People who do what *you* want, not what they want."

"I tried and they just made me feel bad, talking about how I would just be another nameless, faceless Nashville wanna-be country singer if they hadn't—"

"See, that's where you stop them," he says firmly, a scowl darkening his handsome features. "Maybe that's what would have happened, but you're Jade fucking Cantrell—one of the top country artists in the world right now. Doesn't matter what might or might not have happened. It *did* happen. You are where you are. The what ifs are just how they manipulate your emotions."

"Rico said…" I repeat the conversation and he pulls in a sharp breath.

"I'm going to beat the fuck out of him if I ever see him again," he growls. "What the hell?"

"It caught me off-guard too."

"Look, there's an element of truth to what he said—if you shit on people on your way up, it could be problematic if you're ever on your way back down. That said, doing what's best for your business isn't shitting on anyone. He told you he didn't want to produce country anymore—whose fault is it that you took him at his word?" He waits, obviously expecting an answer, and I sigh wearily.

"I know but—"

"There are no buts, Shortcake." He takes my chin between his thumb and forefinger and turns my head, forcing me to look at him. "You've got this. I'm here now. And we're going to handle it. Together."

"Are we?" I stare into his eyes. "Because I honestly have no idea what to do."

"I'm going to help you. I have a fantastic entertainment attorney who will kick ass and take names. A management company who'll take care of you if you decide you want to use them. And maybe even a new record label, depending on what your contract says."

I'm overwhelmed with gratitude and relief and hope.

But there's one thing that's more important than all of that other stuff.

At least, it is to me.

"Will you produce my album?" I blurt. "I let Rico think it was a done deal, but you and I only talked about it in passing. I don't want you to do it because you feel bad about what's been happening—I want you to do it because you want to. That's the only way it works."

"I'm *never* going to do something just because I feel bad," he says with a soft chuckle. "You'll learn that about me pretty quickly. But that's not the case here. I just want to be sure you know what you're asking. Are you positive you want me to produce? I've never done a country album."

"I know, but I trust you. We work well together. It's magic when we're making music." And other things, but I need to focus. "I know the songs we wrote together are going to be huge. Just like I knew 'Forever in Rewind' was going to hit number one. Sometimes I just know. I feel it. And everything inside me tells me you're the right person to produce the next album."

"If you're sure about this, I'd be honored," he says softly, leaning in to press his lips to mine. My mouth opens of its own volition, and our tongues slide together with a magnetic force. And yet, he's not in a rush, not tearing at my clothes or trying to get me naked. Instead, he kisses me like we have all the time in the world. Like kissing me is the only thing he cares about.

"I'm going to take you to bed and make you come at least five times tonight," he whispers against my mouth, "but I want to take care of something first." He pulls his phone out of his pocket. "We're going to talk to Madeline Aronson."

Holy guacamole.

Everyone knows Madeline Aronson.

It doesn't get any more powerful than her as far as entertainment attorneys. It's almost impossible to get a consultation with her, much less hire her full-time, but Royal dials what appears to be a direct number and puts her on speaker.

"Royal!" She answers almost immediately.

"Hey, Maddie."

"Madeline," she corrects him. "How many times do I have to tell you that?"

"Yeah, yeah." He rolls his eyes. "Listen, I'm here with Jade Cantrell. You have a few minutes to talk to her?"

"I have…" She hesitates, as if looking for something. "...thirteen minutes."

"Talk fast," Royal tells me.

"I wasn't prepared," I say, "but hello. It's nice to meet you… *Madeline*."

She laughs. "I like her, Royal."

"Me too," he says.

"Anyway, give me the Reader's Digest version of what's going on," Madeline says.

"Basically, my management company is trying to force me into working with people I don't like and doing things I don't want to do. I need someone to fight some of these battles for me because I can't focus on the creative stuff when I spend hours every day arguing with people who don't have my back. I need someone who knows what's in my contracts, how to potentially get me out of them, and who'll tell me what I can and can't do."

"That's all?" Madeline snorts. "Royal, you said this was hardcore."

"It is," he says firmly. "They're dicking her around and it's becoming problematic. You asked for the condensed version. There have been some veiled threats and about how she wouldn't be where she is without them. Shit like that. It needs to stop."

"Not a problem. Send me over your contracts with your record label and the management company. If you get those to me today, I can talk to you late tomorrow, around eight in the evening Nashville time? Does that work?"

"Absolutely. I'll get you those documents in a little while." I don't even know where the contracts are, but if she can help, I'm more than willing to do my part to hunt them down.

"Great. Royal has my email address." She pauses. "By the way, I'll look at the contracts free of charge as a favor to Royal, but in case you decide to sign with me, I'll be attaching my rate sheet."

"Money isn't an issue," I reply.

"Great. Then we'll talk tomorrow." She disconnects and I turn to Royal, squinting.

"How did you do that?"

"Been around the block a few times," he says patiently. "And anyway, Madeline is good people. She's been my attorney since before the accident, and it's the best decision I ever made. She's a little brusque and won't give you the warm fuzzies, but she's loyal, smart, and incredible at her job. She's expensive but worth every penny."

"She's someone you trust." It's not a question but he answers anyway.

"More than anyone outside of my family."

"I've heard she has a three-year waiting list just for a consultation."

He smiles. "Like I said, I've been doing this a while."

"What if she can't help me?"

"She will. Trust me." He winds his fingers through mine and pulls me onto his lap.

"I do." I rest my head against his chest, and it feels like he's lifted the weight of the world from my shoulders. "I...thank you. I can't tell you how much this means to me."

"You're welcome. Everything is going to be okay. I promise."

When he says it, I believe it.

He's not just some rock star I'm sleeping with; he's quickly becoming extremely important to me. I know I shouldn't be falling in love but it's too late.

And the fact that he's here tells me he's falling too.

It might be the scariest thing that's ever happened to me, but it's also the most incredible thing too.

I can't think of a single thing that feels better than being with him, having his attention focused on me...and falling in love with him.

No matter what happens, I can't imagine regretting a single moment of any of it.

CHAPTER TWENTY-FIVE

Royal

WE TALK with Maddie the next evening and come up with a loose plan to straighten things out—read: to kick those assholes to the ends of the earth and back.

And then again for good measure.

The pieces put into place, we get down to business.

Also known as fucking our way through every room in Jade's house.

I'm a particular fan of the huge island she has in the kitchen—it's the perfect height to bend her over and plunge into her from behind again and again and *again.*

Probably why her cheeks keep flushing pink every time she looks at me as she absently strums on the guitar.

I blink, the memory of her tight cunt clamping around me disappearing when I hear it.

It.

"Stop."

We've been working enough that she doesn't question my sharp interjection.

"This?" she asks, playing something.

Just not the *right* something.

"No."

Her nose wrinkles and she's so fucking cute that I want to lean in and kiss the tip of it. But…work.

An album to produce.

Which means songs to write.

Which means—

"No," I say again when her fingers start moving again, the first chord wrong.

She huffs out a sigh, starts again, her eyes on mine.

I just shake my head.

"Son of a nutcracker," she grumbles, and laughter bubbles up in my chest. Only, it doesn't escape because her fingers are moving again and—

"Yes. *That.*"

Her mouth curves and her eyes soften as she keeps playing and—

"Yes," I say softly. "Yes, Shortcake. Keep going." I sink down behind her, adjust her hands slightly so she can hit the chord progression a little easier. "Just like that, only make that last note a sharp."

She lets my hands guide hers, leaning back against my chest, doing all the fine motor stuff while I help with the stuff that I can actually do.

Which is less than I want.

And more than I thought.

"There," she breathes.

"Yes." I close my eyes as we continue playing, piecing the notes together in that effortless way we seem to have together.

And pretty soon we're strumming through the song and the words are coming and—

"That's perfect," she whispers, the last note hanging in the air.

"Now we just need words," I say dryly.

"You mean my album isn't just going to be an instrumental?"

"Funny." I tug a strand of her hair then nod at her notebook. "Okay, Shortcake, bust out that pen and fancy paper of yours."

"A girl talks *one* time about how nice the ink feels gliding over the page."

"My tongue is the ink," I sing. *"Your skin is the page."*

There that blush goes again, bright red on her cheeks. Her lips parting on a shaking exhale.

But her voice is steady as she strums and sings, *"My desire is forbidden pink. Your kisses are a rage."*

"Damn," I whisper, my cock hardening against my zipper, my arms tightening around her. "Baby, for someone who doesn't curse, that was hot as hell."

She grins up at me, those cheeks still flushed, her storm cloud gray eyes sparking with lightning. With *heat.*

I tug the guitar out of her hands, set it to the side.

"Wh—?"

I kiss her, long and deep and slow, dragging her shirt up and over her head, tossing it to the side so I can peel off her bra, feast on her breasts.

She gasps when I suck a nipple deep, tugs sharply at my hair when I nibble a bit too roughly.

Grinning, I continue kissing her as I slide my hand down her belly, flick open the button of her jeans. I grasp the tag, tug down the zipper, and then I'm slipping my fingers beneath the waistband of her underwear. *Lower.* "Speaking of forbidden pink."

Bright red cheeks.

Slickness coating my skin.

I stroke her, firm and sure, just exactly as she likes. And pretty soon she's rocking against my hand—

"Royal," she whispers.

Close.

Already.

Christ, it's like this woman is meant for me.

That sends a blip of emotion tearing through me—fear and panic, need and *more.*

But then she surprises me, gripping my hand and tugging it out from her pants. "Get naked," she orders breathlessly.

"I love that you're a good girl out there"—I rip my shirt over my head—"but my bad girl in here with me."

"*Royal*."

I grin.

Her chin comes up. "Now, get naked."

It takes seconds to oblige her and I get to enjoy the sight of her tits bouncing as she shoves down her jeans, her underwear, but when she reaches for the pair of ridiculously fuzzy socks, I stop her.

"Leave them." I steal a kiss. "They're fucking adorable. Just like you."

"But they don't exactly scream *bad girl* now, do they?"

"Who says?" I ask as I roll on a condom.

"*I* say—*ack!*"

I grip her hips, drag her on top of me. "Come put those socks to good use, Shortcake."

"How—?"

But I don't give her a chance to overthink it. I just draw her down and flex my hips, thrusting up into her.

We both groan at the tight fit, her head falling back, my control already splintering.

"Fuck me, baby."

She lifts her head, those gray eyes burning into mine, and our gazes lock together as she lifts up and drops down, as she grinds forward, as she takes me deep and fucks me, slow and steady at first, then rough and hard.

"Royal!" she gasps as she clamps around me, coming apart.

And that's enough to send me over the edge.

My orgasm blasts through me as she collapses onto my chest. I grip her hips as my thrusts go wild, hold her close as my pulse settles, inhale the scent of her hair, feel the silk of her skin, the weight of her body, the hot glaze of her breath on my throat.

"Your pulse is the rhythm," she sings softly. *"Your heart the only thing that makes sense."*

"And when I hold you close," I finish, *"I know I'll never let you go."*

"SEE?" Jade says a few days later, linking her hand with mine, her cheeks bright pink, albeit this time from the cold rather than me fucking her senseless.

"See what?" I ask as we stroll along the sidewalk, the small town outside of Nashville filled with small-town appeal.

The downtown has an eclectic charm, the shops lining both sides of the street as varied as their contents—crystal shops next door to cute pet stores, custom jewelry businesses next to tiny hole-in-the-wall restaurants.

"This is nice," she says, swinging our hands back and forth. "Just doing normal things like getting fancy coffee"—she holds up her to go cup—"and window shopping."

It is nice.

Or *was* before I noticed the attention Jade and I are getting. The surreptitious pictures being taken of us, the eyes tracking our movements.

I need to get us out of here before something goes wrong.

We don't have security.

And the greedy eyes of the people tracking us…

It's making my lungs tighten, my vision shrink.

"Royal?" Her stride falters, and she looks up at me. "Are you okay?"

I nod tightly. "I'm great. *This* is great."

"Why do I feel like a but is coming?"

"Look around, Shortcake."

She frowns but dutifully glances from side to side. "I know the shops aren't as nice as the ones in L.A., but—"

"No." I squeeze her hand, ignoring that it's my bad hand, that the sensation is wrong.

That *all* of this is wrong.

"*Look around,* baby."

Her throat works. Then she sighs and drags her stare away from me, pointing it back out to the street.

And another falter in her stride tells me she sees it then.

"Fiddlesticks," she whispers.

"We need to go."

Her eyes come back to mine, and she nods. "We need to go."

We start to turn around when I hear it.

"Jade?"

The child's voice has us both freezing and pivoting back. And there she is, an adorable little girl who's maybe a couple of years older than Frankie. Her parents are behind her, wide smiles on their faces.

"Yes," she says, crouching down and extending her hand. "I'm Jade. What's your name?"

"Calle."

"Hi, Calle." She shakes her hand. "It's nice to meet you."

"Can you sign this for me?"

I'm watching the interaction, smiling slightly as I watch Jade sign a T-shirt that looks to have been bought from one of the nearby shops. But even as I do that, I'm aware of more people closing in.

The tightness in my lungs increases.

Calle's parents snap a picture then wave goodbye. But before I can get Jade out of there, a few other fans come forward. They're respectful and the interactions are brief, so I just stand by as she signs a couple more autographs and takes a few more photos.

But the worry in my stomach is growing.

We *need* to go.

Finally, Jade finishes with the last of her fans, and I move close to her side. "Time to go, Shortcake."

Her eyes hit mine, and I know she picks up on my tension—read: near panic—when she immediately nods and weaves her fingers through mine.

"Let's hit it."

"Got time for one more autograph?"

We both freeze, the hairs on my nape prickling.

The man's tone is off, and more than a little entitled.

But Jade dutifully turns around, scrawls her name on the poster.

"Just one more," the man says as she tries to hand the pen back, reaching into his backpack and pulling out a clipboard with several more memorabilia items.

An autograph reseller.

Ugh. I fucking hate these guys.

"I'm sorry," Jade says, her tone polite but firm. "We're late and need to head out." She slips her arm through mine.

"Seriously?" the man snaps, shoving the clipboard in her face. "You took a century with those dumb little kids, but you can't take two minutes with me?"

"We're going," I tell him, shoving the clipboard away.

"Fuck you."

"Look, man," I say quietly. "She signed that for you, and you'll be able to sell it for plenty of money. So take that as a win and shut the fuck up, all right?"

I glance down at Jade. "Let's—"

A hand grips my shoulder, yanking me back, tearing my hand from Jade's, knocking me back a pace.

She cries out as I regain my balance, and I turn to see the asshole in her face.

Touching her.

My vision is no longer tinged with black.

Instead, it's red.

I shove the fucker away from her. "Touch her again and I'll break it off."

"Fuck off, asshole." He takes a swing at me.

I swing back. Once.

Because it only takes one punch to eliminate the threat.

He staggers and falls back onto the sidewalk, landing hard on his ass.

"Come on," I say, taking Jade's hand as the man rubs his hand over his face, hating all of the cameras pointed in our direction, hating even more that this is going to be all over social media in a matter of minutes.

"Oh, my God," she whispers.

I hate even more that she's trembling.

But I deal with the first problem first.

I get her into the car, point us back in the direction of Nashville.

Then I deal with the second.

I call my crisis control publicist, let her know what just happened.

"That jerk could have hurt me," Jade whispers after I hang up.

"Not as long as I'm still breathing, Shortcake."

And with that, I deal with the third.

"But I can't protect you here." I reach across the console, take her hand, holding tight until she stops trembling enough and looks at me. "We have to go back to L.A., Shortcake."

CHAPTER TWENTY-SIX

Jade

THE LAST FEW days since the incident in Tennessee have been a whirlwind.

The media is completely out of their minds with the idea that country music sweetheart Jade Cantrell is involved with rock and roll bad boy Royal Ewing.

Not to mention him punching out an autograph seeker.

It seems like everyone on the street that day got it on video, but in this case, that's turned out to be a good thing. Anyone watching can clearly see the guy grabbing me and then he swings at Royal first, so at least everyone knows Royal didn't start it.

The whole thing was jarring, and I have to admit I do feel safer here in L.A.

Not only do we have a security team whenever we go anywhere, but Royal has made it clear that he can protect me too. Which is hotter than hot. I'm not a fan of violence, in general, but there's something sweet about the way he reacts when anyone gets near me without my permission.

I'd be lying if I said I didn't like it.

Today, however, is something else entirely.

Sunday Dinner with Royal's family.

I won't even pretend I wasn't intimidated when we first arrived.

Royal doesn't have to spell it out for me to know this is a big deal.

He doesn't bring girls home to the family.

Ever.

And yet, here I am, sitting around a table playing Connect Four with a very competitive three-year-old who isn't planning to go down without a fight.

Her little face is scrunched in concentration, her chin resting on her fist as she levels narrowed eyes in my direction.

"You've played this before," she says, a slightly accusatory tone to her voice.

"I have," I say solemnly. "My grandpa used to play with me when I was your age."

"That's not fair. You've been playing for years." She sighs dramatically.

It's all I can do to bite back my laughter.

She's beyond adorable.

Smart and sassy but also sweet and curious about everything.

And she *adores* her Uncle Royal.

It's incredible to watch them together.

He probably doesn't realize it, but he will make an amazing father.

Which gets my ovaries practically swooning with excitement.

Not that I want a baby any time soon, but Royal's baby?

Oh, yes.

With my light hair, his blue eyes, and definitely his height. And my vocal chords.

It's all I can do not to giggle at the thought.

Except Frankie is waiting for me to make my move.

And when I do, I'm going to win.

I meet Royal's gaze across the table, and he seems to understand my hesitation. He gives me a barely perceptible nod so I go ahead and declare victory. Frankie looks shocked at first, and then to my surprise, everyone starts laughing.

"She lets everyone win the first time they play," Royal whispers, grinning. "Then she moves in for the kill in game two."

I roll my eyes. "Fine. We'll see."

"All right." Briar looks at Frankie. "You need to get cleaned up before dinner and let us adults have a little time with Jade too. You've monopolized her since she arrived."

"But she's my friend!" Frankie protests.

"She's our friend too," her mother responds. "You're going to play guitar for her after dinner, but now, we're going to have grown-up talk."

"Fi-ine." Frankie makes a face but gives in good-naturedly.

"She's so cute," I say when she's taken the Connect Four game back to her room.

"Full of piss and vinegar sometimes," Briar grins, "and she keeps all five of us on our toes."

"Imagine how boring it would be if she didn't," I say.

"There's that," Briar agrees.

"I hope this little one is a little *less* interesting as I get later in my pregnancy," Aspen murmurs, rubbing her belly. "I'm so tired of being nauseated."

"Do you need anything?" Mrs. X asks her. The older woman, who seems like a cross between housekeeper and mother hen, has been bustling around the kitchen, refusing to let any of us help. She's finally sitting down, but I notice how she hovers around Aspen.

Well, they all seem to.

"I'm fine," Aspen says with a soft smile. "I took the antinausea meds because I didn't want to spend the whole day puking in front of poor Jade. Except I forgot how sleepy they make me."

"Don't worry about me," I say, shaking my head. "You can

puke or nap or whatever else you need to do. I'll probably just be in Frankie's room losing at Connect Four anyway."

Everyone chuckles.

Aspen nestles into Banks's side, her eyelids heavy, and I can't help but notice how much love there is in the room. It's almost palpable, the way they care about each other.

I've never had relationships like this one. Not since my grandmother died. But even then, it was different. She loved me to pieces, but she was from a different generation, where she worried about appearances, behavior, manners, and lots of other things that kept her from being physically affectionate.

That's not the case here.

"I'm going to check the brisket and put some bread in the oven," Briar says, giving Mrs. X a look. "You stay right there."

"Yes, ma'am." Mrs. X winks at me as I get up.

"I'll help," I say, following Briar into the kitchen.

"You don't have to do anything," she says over her shoulder. "You should spend time with Royal."

"Royal and I spend plenty of time together." I laugh. "I came here to spend time with all of you."

"I'm sorry if Frankie has been monopolizing your time," she says, pulling a loaf of bread out of the freezer. "She's really excited that you're Royal's *special* friend."

I laugh. "To be fair, I'm kind of excited about that too."

We laugh for a moment before she sobers.

"We've been so worried about him," she says softly. "He hasn't been the same since the accident, and now, finally…well, he seems like himself again. I mean, he won't ever be who he was before, but at least he's living again."

"Wasn't he living before?" I ask curiously.

"Not really. The only time he left the house was to come to family dinner or spend time with Frankie. Occasionally, he'd meet the guys up at The Sapphire Room, but other than that, he was a hermit. It scared me. Scared all of us. But we couldn't seem to reach him." She pauses, smiling again. "And then came you."

I flush. "Well, he's special. I'm sure you already know that."

"I do, but the two of you as a couple caught us by surprise. After Amber—"

She cuts off as Mrs. X comes into the kitchen.

"I'm just here to be nosy," she says before Briar can say anything. "Not to fuss with dinner. Aspen fell asleep so the guys are talking hockey, and you know I'm only good for about two minutes of that slap shot crap before I get bored."

Briar laughs. "That's okay. We were just about done in here. Dinner won't be for another half hour or so."

We head back to the family room, and I pause in front of the fireplace mantel.

"Good golly, Miss Molly, who is *that*?" I ask, staring at a framed picture of an incredibly good-looking man.

"That's Colt," Briar says softly, coming to stand next to me.

Colt.

Royal's friend who died.

The one they honor every year on his birthday.

Whoa Nellie, he was easy on the eyes.

"Well, he was hot," I say.

"He was." Briar is almost wistful as she stares at the picture.

"That Colt was one hell of a tall drink of water," Mrs. X says loudly, playfully fanning herself.

"Ew." Dash makes a face. "Did you just call Colt a tall drink of water?"

"What if I did?" Mrs. X asks, arching a brow. "You think just 'cause I'm old I don't have eyes? I bet the ladies were falling all over themselves to get to him in college."

Banks snorts. "That they were."

"Did he have a girlfriend when he died?" I ask, looking over at the guys.

Atlas shakes his head. "He was way too busy playing the field. He said he never wanted to settle down."

"He just hadn't met the right woman," Mrs. X says. "Someone eventually would have snatched him up."

"Not Colt." Banks shakes his head.

"You realize you used to say the same thing, right?" Dash nudges him.

"Fuck off." He scowls at his friend.

They trade a few insults, and Briar tells them to shut up so they don't wake Aspen.

Royal gets up and comes over to where I'm perusing the rest of the photos on the mantel.

Briar and Frankie at what appears to be a christening ceremony.

Briar, and the guys—all five of them—at her college graduation.

Royal holding Frankie as a newborn.

"When was this?" I ask, pointing to the picture.

He smiles. "She was just a few hours old. I couldn't stop staring at her. Holding her. She was just this perfect, tiny little angel."

"Were you in the delivery room with her?"

He nods. "I was. Her parents were stuck out of the country, and Dash was too grossed out about seeing his sister's vagina to do it. Atlas is too much of a control freak—he knew he couldn't handle seeing her in pain like that. And Banks was on a road trip. Which left me. One of the best moments of my life, watching Frankie come into the world, holding Briar's hand…It was an emotional day, less than six months after Colt died, so we were still pretty raw. Frankie helped us heal." He clears his throat. "I guess she's still helping. Especially with me."

I slide my arm through his. "She's a special little girl. And you're a very special man."

He looks down at me. "If you keep saying stuff like that, I might start to believe you."

"You should." I lean against him, and he wraps an arm around my waist.

"I'm really glad you're here," he says. "With me. With us. Everyone likes you."

"And I like them."

I could get used to being part of a family again.

This family.

Royal's family.

CHAPTER TWENTY-SEVEN

Royal

"THESE ARE REALLY, *REALLY* GOOD," Jade says, finishing off her second Gamebreaker.

Her cheeks are flushed and her lips are swollen. My dick twitches, reminding me of how she looks after I've made her come.

It doesn't help that she's leaning against me, her tits pressed into my arm, her scent in my nose. I want her—*always* want her. But this is good for her. The last week on a whole has been good for her—getting her away from the assholes on her team, setting her up with Maddie, with Kate Martensson, my crisis control publicist, and with Dash, who's taken control of her security.

My house is safe.

Her place in Nashville is getting an overhaul, so it will be safe soon enough.

Maddie and Kate are dealing with Farrah and the record company and the media.

And I'm on Jade duty.

So, we've been spending a lot of time working on her album,

fucking like jackrabbits, and hanging with Frankie, Briar, and whatever mix of the guys are around.

Tonight that's all of them.

Aspen had an early shift and the Vipers aren't playing tonight, so they're both here, Aspen cuddled up next to Banks in our booth, sipping on a glass of Sprite and looking far better than I've seen her in the last couple of months. Maybe the medicine is helping.

She wrinkles her nose and sets down her glass, rubbing at her belly.

Or maybe not.

Atlas slipped out of the noisy bar to take a call in the manager's office. He seems stressed and on edge tonight, as though he's managing more than his normal workload, and as a result, the rest of us have been tiptoeing around him.

Well, the rest of us being the guys.

The girls continue to be themselves, not worried about the brooding bastard in the least.

Banks, Dash, and I, on the other hand, recognize his mood and are walking on eggshells.

Funny, it's usually me that they're worried about.

Funny *not* funny, I guess, considering the pit in my stomach and the concern gnawing at my gut.

Is this what I've put my family through?

My temple throbs, and I rub at the ache, focusing back on this moment and shoving down all of the fucked up shit. I'm getting my head together, figuring out a way to be better. I'm a long fucking way away from perfect, but…

Jade.

I'm different with her.

Maybe I can be a good enough man for her yet.

"Do you want me to get you another?" I ask her, taking the drained glass and setting it on the table next to the abandoned Sprite.

She shakes her head and leans more heavily against me. "No, thanks though, honey. I'll stick with water for a bit."

"You got it."

Her sigh is contented, and I tune out as she, Briar, and Aspen start talking about the shade of lipstick she's wearing, some fancy product from some celebrity's new makeup line. Apparently, it stays on all day.

I plan on testing that later.

Because that shade of red on her lips conjures all sorts of fantasies—stretched wide as I fuck her mouth, parting as she sucks me deep, smeared on my skin as—

My dick twitches again, and I grit my teeth.

This is about family, not fucking.

I exhale silently, see that Dash has gotten bored with the conversation about lipstick and made his way to the bar. He's talking with a woman, his smile wide and his laugh loud, though it doesn't seem as though she's giving him the time of day as he tries to chat her up.

Something the girls have noticed too.

Jade winces as he's obviously turned down, even from a distance.

Briar is rolling with laughter at the sight of her brother striking out, and Aspen is nudging at Banks's side, teasing him, "What is it with all of The Gamebreakers striking out in the bar you guys own?"

"For one thing," Banks says, brushing back her hair and studying her face like he's trying to memorize every facet of it, "it's not a *bar*."

"No, it isn't," Dash says, scowling as he drops down into the booth next to me, his long legs sprawled out in front of him.

"For another," Banks says dryly, drawing Aspen even closer, "I don't think winning over the woman I love can be considered *striking out*."

"And I don't think that one"—Briar nods at the woman Dash was hitting on and we all turn to see her sling her arm around another woman's shoulders then kiss her deeply—"is for my brother."

Jade's mouth falls open. "Holy baloney, *that's* a kiss."

I nip at the top of her ear, my next words for her ears only. "Okay, Shortcake, now *I'm* insulted."

Her cheeks go pink, and she turns to me, settling her hand on my chest. "I didn't mean that you—I mean, *we*—" Pink turning to red, her mouth opening and closing a few times, like an adorable fish. "I mean, *you*—" Then her eyes sharpen and she swats me lightly on the chest as she clues in that I'm teasing her. "Royal-pain-in-the-butt! How dare you?"

The table freezes.

Then breaks out into laughter.

Briar is almost bent in half, nearly spilling the one drink she allows herself before she has to go and relieve Mrs. X from her babysitting duties.

Banks and Aspen hold on to each other as they cackle.

Dash's big guffaw makes it clear he's not worried about striking out, especially as he shrugs and slings his arm across the back of the booth. "Who knows?" he says. "They could be open to a third."

I roll my eyes and unleash my strongest, most powerful glare on all of them.

"That nickname better not see the light of day," I threaten.

Briar straightens, leaning over and clapping me on the shoulder. "Give it up, Royal-pain-in-the-butt. We're immune to your glares, and that nickname is here to stay."

I stifle my groan, turn my glare to Jade. "This is your fault."

Her hand on my chest slides up to cup my jaw, and a sliver of pride slides through me when she leans up and slants her mouth over mine, kissing the fuck out of me.

This isn't a woman who's ashamed to be seen with me.

"Woo, mama," I hear distantly, and realize that Briar has stopped laughing at me and is now fanning herself. "Talk about a *kiss.*"

"I think we should go home," Aspen says, trailing her hand down Banks's chest. "Like *right* now."

"Jesus, brother," Dash mutters. "Get a fucking room."

"Going home works for me," Banks says, dragging Aspen even closer.

"Oh, my God," Jade murmurs, her blush growing to astronomical proportions. But before I can remind her that I fucking *love* it when she's a siren between the sheets, Atlas reappears, and one look at his face has cold gripping my insides and squeezing tightly.

"What is it?" I rasp.

"You two need to come with me."

He doesn't give me a chance to ask for an explanation—he's spinning on his heel and marching across the floor, the crowd parting for him as he disappears down the hallway.

"What's going on?" Briar asks.

I shake my head, flicking my gaze to hers for a heartbeat. "I don't know." I stand up, reach down and take Jade's hand, drawing her to her feet. "But we're going to find out."

Jade and I hurry after him, finding him standing in the open door of the manager's office.

"Sit down," he orders, closing it behind us then moving to the desk, perching on the edge of it. "First, know that there is no fucking way that I'm going to let this stand. I've already got my legal team working on it, and they'll coordinate with your team on best steps forward."

Jade begins trembling as she settles in one of the open chairs. "P-please just tell me what's happening."

Atlas exhales. "It's not going to be pretty, Jade. You'll need to brace yourself."

That trembling becomes shaking, and I drag her chair closer, take her hand. "Breathe," I order softly then glance up at Atlas, silently telling him to stop fucking around.

I don't say it out loud though.

Because the look in his eyes…

Fuck, this is going to be really bad, isn't it?

He pushes off the desk and crouches in front of us. Then pulls out his phone, taps at the screen, and holds it up as the last notes of "Midnight Snow" begin to play.

Show me the moon and I'll give you the stars
Baby, you know me, and this night is ours…

MY BROWS DRAG TOGETHER.

Okay, so the song leaked. That sucks, but it's not the end of the world.

Then I hear it.

The *really bad* part.

There's a rustle, a moan, and…

"Fuck, Jade," I hear myself whisper on the recording. "You are so fucking beautiful."

She moans. "*Please*. I need you, Royal. I—"

Atlas taps at his screen again and the recording cuts off.

There's a long, tense moment of quiet…

And then Jade bursts into tears.

CHAPTER TWENTY-EIGHT

Jade

I've never been so embarrassed.

Or humiliated.

Or emotional.

And if Atlas has heard the recording, then the rest of the world has too.

Which is horrifying.

Grandma Louise would be so upset with me right now.

I don't know how this happened unless—

My head snaps up.

No-no-*no*.

Now I'm as furious as I am humiliated.

"What is it?" Royal asks softly, watching my face.

"Darn it!" I burst into tears all over again. "This is my fault. Oh my God, I'm so sorry!"

"Hey, it's okay. Jade…baby." Royal does that thing I love, where he grabs my chin between two fingers and forces me to look at him. "It's not the end of the world, okay? We'll get this taken care of. I promise."

"How? It's not like it's fake!" I shudder against him. "I'm so sorry…"

"Tell us what happened," Atlas says in his scary-but-I'm-not-scared-of-him voice. The murderous glare has actually softened. Just a tiny bit. Softer for Atlas anyway.

"I remember that night," Royal ponders thoughtfully. "We wound up making love in the middle of working on the song—I guess we left the recording on?"

"We did." I nod miserably, my face still incredibly hot. I can't remember the last time I blushed as much as I have since meeting Royal. "I didn't realize it at the time but then later, when I found it, I decided to keep it." My face might be competing for the surface of the sun in temperature. So, so hot. I can't even look at Atlas, but even if I wanted to ask him to leave the room, what would that accomplish? He's obviously already heard everything.

And he's trying to help.

Not that you can put a genie back in the bottle.

This is out in the world.

My millions of fans have heard me—

Nope.

I can't even think about all the little girls out there who adore me, listening to me having a very loud, boisterous orgasm.

"How come?" Royal's voice is soft, his eyes boring into mine, breaking into my haze of self-flagellation.

"Because I'm falling in love with you and I love your voice when we…" I let myself trail because Atlas doesn't need to hear any more detail than that and—

Royal presses his forehead to mine.

"I like it too," he whispers. "And I'm sorry this happened. Do you know how it got out? Did you share it with someone?"

I nod, still miserable.

"Not intentionally but I'm pretty sure I know when it happened. When Rico came over. I was so excited to play 'Midnight Snow' for him. I must've sent him the wrong file—you and

I made so many recordings that weekend." I pull out my phone and start scrolling through our texts. "Yup. Right there." I sigh and close my eyes. "I'm so, so sorry. I can't blame anyone but myself. How could I be so stupid?"

"Look, if it was just me, I'd be laughing my ass off right now," Royal says firmly. "Seriously, babe. If you're worried about *my* reputation, please don't apologize. All I care about is how embarrassed you are. People can think whatever the fuck they want about me. And frankly, I'm never going to apologize for hot, consensual sex with a beautiful woman. There's nothing wrong with what we're doing on that tape."

Atlas has somehow managed to make himself as unobtrusive as possible, surreptitiously handing me a couple of tissues.

"Thank you." I blow my nose and dab at my eyes.

God, I must be a mess.

"My legal team is on it, and once we coordinate with yours, this will go away." Fierce, scary Atlas is back, but he's the last person I'm afraid of right now.

"I'm going to text Maddie," Royal says, pulling out his phone.

I don't have the energy or mental bandwidth to do anything but stare off at nothing.

How could I have done something so stupid? Reckless?

Old Rico, the Rico I thought I knew, would have laughed his ass off and immediately deleted it, telling me to be more careful. Reminding me that there are a lot of crazies in the music industry.

That Rico doesn't exist, though.

That Rico was friends with a Jade who hadn't won Song of the Year.

Award-winning Jade apparently doesn't have any friends.

Other than a handful of people in this club right now.

How have I allowed myself to become so isolated?

I'm incredibly grateful for Royal and this newfound friendship with his family, but that doesn't excuse me from putting myself in this position. At some point, I have to think about that.

"Maddie's calling," Royal says, putting her on speaker phone.

"What the hell is going on?" she demands.

Royal introduces her to Atlas, and they have a conversation like Royal and I aren't even here.

"We should bring Kate in on this," Maddie says. "Hang on, let me add her to the call."

A moment later, Kate's voice fills the room.

"I'm sorry to bother you this late at night," Royal tells her.

"That's what I'm here for," she says. "My husband and I just got back from a day at an indoor water park with the twins—so I might be out of the loop. What's going on?"

"Hang on, let me text you something," Madeline tells her.

Ugh.

How many more people are going to hear that recording?

Oh, wait.

The whole freakin' world.

My face flames all over again.

"It's going to be okay," Royal whispers. "Breathe."

"Ohhh." Kate's voice is all business now. "Okay. So this is bad, but not horrible."

Not horrible?

Easy for her to say.

"What do you suggest?" Madeline asks her. "From a crisis control standpoint. We'll handle the legalities."

"At the end of the day, there's nothing we can do. The recording is real, not doctored or made with AI. And if there's proof that Jade knowingly sent him the recording, even if it was by accident, you can't go after him that way. The best course of action is to take ownership."

"Take ownership?" Royal repeats, glaring at the phone. "What does that mean?"

"It means, if we behave as though we've done nothing wrong, people will believe it. Ooopsie, that wasn't meant for the public. But we're so in love...and we're working on new music. Guess what? 'Midnight Snow' is coming out on Valentine's Day—how do you guys feel about new music from Jade Cantrell and Royal Ewing? You know, that kind of thing. Otherwise, we feed into the narrative that the two of you making love is dirty, wrong somehow."

The room is eerily quiet.

"I don't like it," Atlas snaps.

"Atlas." Madeline's voice is patient. "Sit back and think for a moment. This is what Kate does. There is no one better in the entertainment industry for this type of thing. If you, or anyone else, has a better idea, let's hear it."

And of course, they don't.

"I'm fine with it," Royal says abruptly. "I am not ashamed that I make love to my girlfriend. Yes, we apologize for the mistake, but when it's all said and done, we didn't mean any harm. It was supposed to be a text between friends, not some dickhead trying to get her back for not hiring him to produce her next album."

"Ohhh." Kate's voice fills with glee. "No one told me *that* part. Yay! This is awesome. I will vilify Rico in the press. Leave this to me. I'm going to write a statement, okay? All the things I talked about a second ago, and you two can sign off on it. There will be an apology, but only because she never wanted to embarrass her young fan base with something like that. We're not apologizing for being in love and having sex—just that something so private got out. Period."

"I love this," Madeline says. "Royal? Jade?"

I can't formulate a response just yet, but I'm nodding.

This *is* the best course of action.

Of course it is.

I hate it but I've been around long enough to understand how these things work.

"Just, you know, maybe not Valentine's Day for the release of 'Midnight Snow,'" Royal says. "It seems really soon…"

"Why not?" I ask slowly, the idea starting to take root. "We can record it. It's done. I'm sure we can find some musicians to play on it—my drummer, Wayne, is always available, and we can get studio musicians for anything else. It's actually brilliant marketing."

Royal looks startled for a moment but then nods. "Yeah, okay. I guess Valentine's Day can work."

"I still don't know if I like this," Atlas mutters.

"It's okay, big guy," Madeline soothes. "You and I will have a little chat one-on-one and you'll feel better."

He nods even though she obviously can't see it.

Wow.

I love that there's someone out there who can manage Atlas.

I really can't wait to meet Madeline in person.

"All right, the twins need baths, and then their Dad can feed them while I start working on this," Kate says. "Are we good with the plan? I'd like to get this statement out as soon as possible."

"Yes, and we'll check in tomorrow." Madeline is all business again, her soothing tone gone.

"So we're just going to let them get away with this?" Atlas demands.

"Not at all." Soothing Madeline is back. "We're going to sue the fuck out of Rico. But we can't stop the people who've already heard it from listening, downloading…so we spin the narrative. And what are they going to say? Two adults who are in a relationship had sex and recorded it. Big fucking deal."

"Jade's reputation is predicated on her *not* doing things like that," Atlas protests. "This makes her look—"

"Like a grown woman with a boyfriend," Kate interrupts gently.

"We're going to make Rico pay," Madeline says. "And behind the scenes, we're going to get the audio taken down. A good cyber security firm can start working on that, but it takes time. Short-term, we're apologizing for allowing it to get out, but hey, there's a new song coming out on Valentine's Day. Let's focus on that."

They talk for a few more minutes but I'm distracted now.

"Midnight Snow" is releasing on Valentine's Day.

Holy crap.

Royal and I are not theoretically working on a new album with no release date or album title or anything else.

This is a real-life roller coaster ride.

And all I can do now is hold on for dear life.

CHAPTER TWENTY-NINE

Royal

HER HAND IS STILL TREMBLING as we walk out of the office, but her expression is calm.

Hell, considering the blow she's just taken, she's remarkably together.

Wiping her tears, getting on board with a plan, walking back out here with her head held high.

"Everything okay?" Briar asks as we approach the table.

"Not really," I mutter, and watch the alarm sweep across her face. I put up a hand. "I'll fill you in later. For now, I want to get Jade home."

"I'm all right," she says, her fingers squeezing around mine.

Around my bad hand.

And for once, it doesn't feel wrong.

"We can stay until you're ready to go."

I press a kiss to the top of her head, draw her closer. "We're going."

"I—"

"We're *going*."

She huffs out a sigh, shakes her head, but I don't miss the relief that creeps into her beautiful gray eyes.

Dash stands up, his affable, careless playboy demeanor immediately shifting to work mode. "Let's call your team," he says quietly. "Get your car right at the back door and get you two home."

"Th-thanks, Hudson," Jade murmurs.

"Dash," he corrects gently, lightly squeezing her arm. "Remember? All my friends call me Dash."

More emotions in those gray eyes—happiness and hurt, pleasure and reticence, joy and sadness.

"Dash," she corrects, her voice quiet.

He tugs at a strand of her hair. "You guys hang here while I call the crew." His eyes meet mine and then he flicks them to the side.

I get the silent message, and so does Briar.

"Jade," she says, holding up her phone. "Was this the shade of lipstick we were talking about earlier?"

"I—"

"I'll be right back," I tell her, nudging her toward the booth.

"I—"

I cup her jaw. "Just a minute, Shortcake, okay?"

Her lips part on a shaky exhale, but then she nods and joins Aspen and Briar in the booth, Banks slipping out to join us.

Dash tilts his head toward the hall, and we both silently follow him.

"Fill me in." It's the brusque order of a man whose life is this business, so I don't hesitate to tell him what's happened, the skeleton of what our plan is. Banks is listening closely too, but I don't hold anything back. I trust him with my life, and if said life's about to hit the shitter—in the media, that is—then it's good for him to be aware.

God, the last thing I need is for some asshole sports blogger with a bone to pick to surprise him with a question about the tape during a game.

"Damn," Dash says. "Nice friend of hers."

"We're going to bury him." Or, well, Atlas, Maddie, and Kate are, but I'm going to pay them very well to make sure it's properly done.

"Can't wait," he mutters, then sighs and claps me on the shoulder. "Anything you need, man. Anytime."

There's an odd tight feeling in my chest.

I've been such a fuckup, such an asshole.

Taking my family for granted, avoiding them whenever I could, content to sit in my misery.

And they—

Well, they refused to let me remain in the darkness, and they held tight when I was determined to fall.

But it was Jade who pulled me out.

I'm not fucking going back.

Not when she's become my world.

"Thank you," I rasp.

He nods, lifts his phone to his ear, and I hear him barking out orders.

First Atlas. Then Dash.

Banks bumps his shoulder against mine. "Let's get you back to Jade."

I nod, start walking. "Banksy?"

He looks over at me. "Yeah?"

"Thank you."

"I didn't do anything."

"Yeah," I mutter. "You did. You *have*."

Understanding slides through his expression, and he exhales. Then he squeezes me roughly on the shoulder. "You're family." A tilt of his head to Jade. "And she is too. We'll close ranks, keep her safe."

I know they will—though that doesn't make the tightness in my chest go away.

But it makes it bearable.

Because Jade is the most important thing in my life—more

than avoiding the press, more than music, more than my fucking hand not working properly, more than…

Everything.

"Th—"

His fingers on my shoulder tighten. "No thanks needed." His eyes pierce into mine. "Not *ever.*"

I close my eyes, just for a heartbeat, then open them again. "I need to get back to Jade."

He drops his hand, and then we're both exiting the hallway, moving back over to the table.

I don't make it there, though, because when I'm less than five feet away, a hand grips my arm and drags me to a halt.

Wrong—the touch is completely wrong.

Long nails dig into my skin.

Expensive perfume clogs my nose.

Fake tits press into my arm.

What the *fuck?*

"Royal, darling, is that you?"

The voice is nails on a chalkboard and a bucket of ice cold water dumped over me, all at once.

Banks curses and I slowly spin to face her.

Amber.

Christ, she looks even more plastic than before—still beautiful, but any of the soft beauty she once had has been replaced by fillers and Botox. Objectively gorgeous, but I prefer a certain petite brunette with a sprinkle of freckles across the bridge of her nose.

"I'm pretty sure I didn't approve your membership," I say dryly, brushing her hand away and taking a deliberate step back.

"I *know* we didn't," Banks mutters.

"Well, no matter," Amber says. "I don't have a membership." She waves a hand nonchalantly through the air. "My boyfriend does."

"Great." I turn away from her, lock eyes with Jade.

"Aren't you even curious about who I'm with?" she asks. "I mean, I used to be your wife and all."

I glance at her over my shoulder. "I stopped caring about who you fuck when you divorced my crippled ass."

She waves her hand again, as though those words were a small detail.

And fuck, I forgot how much I used to hate when she did that.

"I thought you'd be overjoyed that I found someone worthy of me," she drawls.

"You thought wrong."

Her eyes are calculating, but I don't have time to deal with her particular brand of bullshit today. I start for the table again.

"I don't think I'm wrong."

The calculation has reached her voice now, and my lungs grow tight, my stomach knots. When she gets like this…she's mean as a snake.

I need to get Jade the fuck out of here.

Now.

But my feet aren't obeying that thought.

Slowly, I turn back to face her.

Amber's smile is—

Decidedly snake-like.

And, of fucking course, that's exactly when I feel Jade's hand slide into mine, the contrast between her touch and Amber's as she comes close, as she presses into my side almost comical.

Right and wrong.

Amber's dark brown eyes slide to the side, drift down, and her smile widens. "Who's this?" she asks, as though talking about a child or a dog.

"I'm Jade Cantrell." She sticks out her hand.

Amber doesn't shake it, just wrinkles her nose slightly as she eyes her up and down. Then she glances back at me. "You're dating country bumpkins now?"

"Classic, Amber," I snap, drawing Jade closer. "Spreading your venom everywhere." I meet Jade's eyes. "Let's go."

She nods, but her feet don't move.

Instead, she glares over at Amber.

"You had the most precious gift in the world," she says, "and you squandered it."

My heart pulses.

But I don't have time to respond to that, to kiss her, to tell her what that means to me.

Because Amber splashes some more of that venom around.

"Ah, there you are, baby," she croons and I watch as she plasters herself against—fucking hell, is that Tony Blackthorn? She kisses him with enough tongue that Banks makes a sound of disgust from next to me. "I was just telling them the good news."

I don't bite.

She wants me to know, wants to fuck with me, wants to hurt me.

"About the baby?" he asks, smoothing his hand over Amber's still flat stomach.

I go still, that cold sliding down my spine again.

We were trying for a baby when she…

I grind my teeth together.

When she *left*.

"Congrats," I mutter. "I'm sure you'll be great parents." My sarcasm is about as evident as her venom, and I know she clocks it because her eyes narrow and her cold ass smile spreads. But before she can retort, Tony tugs her against him and proceeds to shove his tongue down her throat.

"Gross," Jade whispers.

"I wasn't *just* telling them about the baby," Amber says coyly after they finally break apart.

That snaps me out of it, and I turn to the woman I want to spend the rest of my life with—and in case anyone is wondering, that's sure as shit *not* the woman who was tongue fucking a sleezy guitar player with a rap sheet a mile long and a trail of NDAs signed in his wake.

It's Jade.

"Let's go," I tell her again.

She nods and we turn to leave.

But Amber's not done with us yet.

"Oh Royal, darling…"

My stomach sinks, but I start walking, *keep* walking, even though her next words are a vicious blow that nearly takes me to my knees.

"Don't you want to meet the new guitarist of Midnight Sun?"

CHAPTER THIRTY

Jade

I DON'T KNOW what's going on with Royal, but seeing his ex-wife impacted him a lot more than I thought it would. It probably has more to do with her dating his replacement—and the fact that no one told him he'd *been* replaced—but I'm not sure what he's feeling because he's been sullen and withdrawn for two days.

We'd finally found our groove as a couple, and this is a setback I hadn't anticipated.

And I can't tell what bothered him more—the sex tape or Amber.

I just...I don't think it's the tape.

He was all about comforting me, on board with the plan that Kate and Madeline came up with until...Amber.

I sigh because I truly don't know if what's eating at him is that Amber is marrying the guy who's replacing him, that she's pregnant, or that she mocked him for being with a country bumpkin like me.

All of the above, I guess.

Because the whole situation seems to be causing him to spiral in a way I don't understand. I haven't seen this side of him before.

The worst part is that I don't know how to pull him out of the darkness that seems to be engulfing him.

The tape threw him for a loop. Seeing Amber another. Learning that she's pregnant one more. And finding out that he's no longer a member of Midnight Sun? About a million loops—enough to make *me* spend far too much time in my head.

So, it's understandable he'd withdraw—especially considering he's not good at emotions.

But…is it really all of that?

Or is it something more?

Something about losing Amber?

No. I don't think he still loves her. Rather, she hurt him in a way only someone you've been completely intimate with can.

And I hate her for it.

She had no business—no *right*—to say the things she said. I don't even care much about what she said about me. People have said worse. Heck, they *are* saying worse. About the sex tape, about my music, about me scraping the bottom of the barrel by dating a washed-up recluse like Royal.

I can't care less about that.

But her pushing him back to the darkness I've worked so hard to bring him out of?

I'll never forgive her for that.

We haven't worked on our music since that night at the Sapphire Room, and when I mention it, he gets defensive.

Like now.

We've just finished breakfast, and I'm putting the dishes in the dishwasher while he sits at the island, ignoring me.

He's definitely not himself.

"Do you want to go to the studio today?" I ask lightly. "We have the time booked—it shouldn't go to waste."

"Not in the mood," he mutters.

"Babe, the album is almost done. I thought you were excited."

He doesn't respond, and my patience is starting to wear thin.

I'm *trying*.

I've been supportive and sweet and thoughtful.

I've attempted to get him to open up without nagging or pushing too hard. But at some point, he has to meet me at least in the ballpark of halfway.

"Royal?"

He's doing something on his phone, completely ignoring me, and his behavior is starting to get irritating.

"I'm just tired, okay?" He doesn't even look up.

"It's eleven o'clock in the morning…and we just got up an hour ago. How tired can you be?"

He chuckles but it hits a bitter note and hangs in the space between us. "We were up pretty late, if I recall."

"We were," I admit, "but I don't think—"

"Let's go back to bed," he murmurs, abruptly standing up and coming over to circle my waist with his right arm, using it to draw me against him.

I know he's deflecting, but this is too important to let him get away with it.

"I don't want to go back to bed just yet," I respond gently, turning to gaze up at him. "I want you to tell me what's bothering you."

He knits his brows together, his blue eyes darkening.

And not in that sexy alpha way I love.

There's annoyance in those fathomless pits, something he rarely shows when we're together.

"We don't have to talk about fucking everything," he snaps. "Okay? I'm allowed to have thoughts that I don't want to share."

I know he's upset.

I know seeing his replacement with Amber had to hurt.

I can only imagine how hard it must be to find out you've

been replaced in the band you started without warning—but none of that is my fault.

We're supposed to be a team, both personally and professionally.

He promised we were in this together.

But it hasn't felt like it the last couple of days, so I'm trying my hardest to be supportive, even though I've felt incredibly alone.

"Of course you are," I say gently, "but it might help to get it off your chest. That's all."

"That's not how I roll, so leave it alone, okay? Please?"

I sigh. "Fine. But I'm going to the studio today. Come with me. It'll get your mind off things. We can just play around with some of the songs we're not sure we're going to use. That's been fun."

"Fun for you maybe." His voice is barely discernible, but I hear it.

And I freeze, staring at him in confusion.

"What does that mean?"

"Nothing. Never mind." He turns away, like he's going to leave the kitchen, but I grab his arm and the questions pour out of me.

"Babe, what's wrong? Do you not want to do the album together anymore? What's going on with you? I understand that scene with Amber was rough, but why are you taking it out on me?"

A tic in his jaw is working overtime, and he doesn't meet my gaze.

The silence grows, a strange, uncomfortable distance between us even though we're only standing a few inches apart.

Frustration hits me like hurricane-force winds, and I put my hands on my hips. "If you have something to say, go ahead and say it!" I snap, losing my temper.

He finally looks up, his face a mask of nothingness.

"Do you have any idea what a step down it is for me to go

from the biggest rock band in the world to working on some country bumpkin-style album?"

I'm not sure how I'm supposed to respond to that, but in the moment, I'm equal parts heartbroken and furious. The woman falling in love with him can't believe he would say something so hurtful, while the country music star who just won a huge award is about to tell him where to stuff it.

"Are you kidding me right now?" I demand.

I have and would put up with a lot because I think he's worth it, but this hurts me in a way I can't describe. If he doesn't think my music is worthy, that's his prerogative, but I refuse to be with a man who talks down to me.

"Do you have any idea what it's like to play an arena with a hundred and fifty thousand people screaming your name?" he asks quietly, fists clenched at his sides. "To be on the fucking top of the world and then have it all come crashing down? Your career, your marriage, your fucking ability to play music? Do you, Jade? Because if not, you can't possibly understand what I'm going through."

"No," I respond tightly, fighting back tears that I truly don't want him to see. "I don't. And I hate everything that's happened to you. But you don't get to hurt all the people around you just because someone else hurt you. That's beneath you. And I deserve better from you."

"Why? Because we're fucking or because I wrote you a song that finally put you on the map?"

Before I can stop myself, I reach out and slap him across the face.

There's a long moment of startled silence. I've never slapped anyone in my life, and my first inclination is to apologize.

But he owes me one first.

"You did *not* put me on the map," I hiss, those blasted tears pushing their way to the surface no matter how hard I try to stop them. "I was a star long before your stupid song…" My voice is starting to break but I refuse to back down. "And you know what else? I'll *still* be a star when you go back to hiding behind your insecurities."

"Yeah, whatever."

"And one more thing," I say, swiping at the tears streaming down my face and throwing down the dish towel I'm still holding as I head for the bedroom to get my things. "Fuck you, Royal Ewing."

CHAPTER THIRTY-ONE

Royal

THE CALL RINGS once and goes straight to voicemail.

Again.

"Fuck," I mutter and toss my phone onto the kitchen island.

The same island I sat at while fucking up my life and hurting a person I love.

Again.

I sigh, shove a hand through my hair, resisting the urge to tear it from my scalp. It's the least I deserve.

But Jade likes my hair.

"Christ." I exhale and push off the stool, trying to find something to occupy my mind. I can't even brood properly—every thought goes to Jade, to that awful conversation and the fucked up things I said and the way they made her eyes change, her expression shift, her shoulders slump, the curse word to slip from her mouth.

I did that.

Hating myself, I grab a beer from the fridge, but when I go to take the bottle opener out of the drawer, I can't help but think about Jade again.

She'd teased me about my bachelor kitchen as she looked for the right kind of measuring cup while baking me the best pumpkin bread I've had, hands down, in my life.

I slam the door shut, put the beer back.

But as I storm out into the hall, my eyes catch on the denim jacket hanging over the banister, bunched up at the bottom of the stairs and forgotten when Jade packed up her stuff and hauled ass out of here.

Not that I blame her.

I was—*am*—an asshole.

But I can't apologize to her if she won't talk to me.

I've been all the fuck over L.A. and haven't been able to track her down.

She's not in Nashville—that was one fucking expensive plane ride—and she's not even in Tahoe.

I know she's safe.

Maddie told me that much.

But the rest of it?

Like where she is, what she's doing, if she's okay—and how can she possibly be okay?

Maddie all but told me to fuck right off when I asked.

Same as Kate.

I stop by that jacket, lifting it from the railing and bringing it to my nose, inhaling deeply. I already know it still smells like her because I've been huffing it like an addict trying to get the last grain of coke off a mirror.

Flowers and vanilla and a hint of something that is unique to Jade hits my senses.

But when I inhale again, I know I have to put an end to my patheticness. I can't keep avoiding the living room because we made a breakthrough there on the chorus of "Nobody's Business"—one of the soulful ballads that's supposed to go on her new album.

It's good enough to be a single.

Not as good as "Midnight Snow," though.

I don't go into the living room—I can't, even though I know I'm a pussy because of it. Instead, I start for my office, but stop a step in, grinding my teeth together so tightly that a bolt of pain shoots through my jaw.

"Dammit." I growl, tossing the jacket back onto the banister, knowing that it won't be long before I'm standing in this exact spot again, huffing at her jacket like a creep.

I can't go into my office either.

Not when the memory of bending her over my desk and fucking her from behind until she came apart on my dick is burned into my mind.

Frankie!

I'll go and play *Connect Four* with my niece until my eyes ache, teach her something new on her guitar. She's ready for something harder.

"Bad Moon Rising" by Creedence Clearwater only has three chords.

She can totally pull that off...and it'll take an extra-long lesson with me focusing on something that isn't Jade and my complete and total fuck-up.

Right.

Good plan.

So much better than standing here at the bottom of the stairs, thinking about how Jade smiled up at me as I carried her to bed, her eyes half-mast and sleepy, her expression full of...love.

That I stomped on.

"Enough," I grit, spinning on my heel and heading for the garage. I snag my keys from the hook mounted by the door and get in my car.

But it's not until I'm almost at Briar's place that I remember what day it is.

Frankie has gymnastics today.

I'm close enough that I finish the drive, go to the door, and use my code to let myself in, hoping against hope that I'll hear Frankie's adorable little voice echoing down the hall.

Unfortunately, it's silent.

I still make a circuit, anyway, and in the process, I help myself to a cookie cooling on a rack in the kitchen.

It's delicious…until I remember Jade's cookies.

Then it sits like lead in my stomach.

I'm pathetic and fully aware of it—and that point is driven home even harder when my phone buzzes as I'm walking out the front door.

I shove my hand in my pocket, practically tearing the fabric as I yank it free.

And I can't hide my disappointment when I see that it's not Jade texting me.

It's Briar, who's clearly spotted me on the security cameras.

She isn't done either, considering that another text comes in right afterward.

BRIAR: I don't believe I gave assholes permission to enter my house.

BRIAR: I'd almost feel sorry for that pathetic expression on your face, if you hadn't been such a dick to Jade.

ROYAL: Never stopped you before.

I suck in a breath, hit the button to engage the lock to the front door, and turn for my car in the driveway. But as I'm walking, I can't stop my fingers from moving on the keyboard, thumbing out another text to Briar before I tug open the driver's side door.

ROYAL: She told you?

BRIAR: We knew things weren't great after the tape broke and Amber's scene at The Sapphire Room. But Aspen and I took her for a spa day and pried it out of her. We thought you two were holed up together, trying to get a handle on everything. Never in a million years did I think you'd be dumb enough to hurt the woman you love, especially like that.

Love.

Love.

Jade had said it, and I hadn't reacted. Because it felt right, just like every other moment with her has.

Because I knew even then that I love her too.

Of course, I do.

How can I not?

And I hurt her.

Pain ricochets through me, slicing deep and without quarter. I deserve it. Hell, I deserve so much fucking *more* than that.

But how do I fix it?

I insulted her music, her professionalism, and worst of all, I hurt her and pushed her away after I had promised—fucking *promised*—to deal with this shitstorm together.

Panic grips my insides, far more intensely than any of the episodes I've experienced since my accident. I can't breathe, can't see because the black has intruded so far in from the edges of my vision that it's blinding.

And I can't think.

Or can't think of anything aside from the fact that I hurt her.

Sweat drips down my spine. My hands spasms on the steering wheel. Mind racing, lungs straining, I drop my forehead to the steering wheel and wait.

I need to fix this.

I need to find a way to make it right.

I need to find *Jade.*

That, thankfully, helps me crawl out of the panic. A first step unclenches the hand wrapped around my heart, finally loosens the tight shackles that prevent my lungs from drawing in enough air.

Eventually, I'm able to remember how to breathe, to get enough oxygen into my body that my mind begins to clear.

I yank a napkin from the glovebox, wipe my face, my hands.

My cell buzzes.

BRIAR: It's not too late to fix it.

I don't respond to her message.

I should, considering that Briar is one of the most important people in my life and has been by my side through thick and thin.

But I don't.

Because I owe Jade the first explanation. No, the first apology.

No, I owe the woman I love something that will prove to her exactly how much I know I fucked up, exactly how much she means to me, exactly the lengths I will go to make things right.

Jade deserves the world.

Not a washed-up rock star too miserable for his own good.

So, no. I don't respond to Briar.

And I don't try to text or call Jade again.

Instead, I back out of the driveway and go to the one person I know has his finger on the pulse of exactly where Jade is.

Dash.

Or Dash's *office*.

He scowls at me as he tugs open the door, and I'm not dumb enough to miss that he doesn't invite me in.

"Is she here?" I rasp.

His hazel eyes are molten with rage. "She's not here," he growls. "Not that I would tell you if she was, asshole."

I don't bother getting mad back.

I deserve that rage.

And it doesn't help me make this right.

"I fucked up," I admit. "I know that, man. I just..." I grind my teeth together, every instinct hating that I need to lay it on the line, even as every instinct is telling me I *need* to lay it on the line. "I fucked up bad. But she blocked me and she isn't home and..."

Dash's face has gone blank and I sigh.

"I can't fix it if I don't know where she is. I've been to Nashville, to Tahoe. I've called Kate and Maddie and even her fucking record company. No one is talking to me." He snorts and I ignore it, pushing on. "I'm begging you, man. I'm *begging* you to tell me where she is."

There's a long pause.

Long enough that the panic begins to edge in again.

Then he says, "I can't."

Just *I can't.*

Panic is replaced by frustration. "You can but you won't."

Another pause, but this one isn't nearly as long. "You're right." He steps out of the opening, begins to close the door, but it's not shut all the way when he strikes the final blow.

"You fucked up. It's up to you to fix it."

CHAPTER THIRTY-TWO

Jade

MISERY.

That's the only word that comes to mind in the days following leaving Royal.

I've had a broken heart before, but nothing has ever felt quite this…miserable.

I'm not just sad, I literally feel shattered. Like something inside of me will never be the same.

I *trusted* him.

Showed him every part of me and he just stomped all over my soul.

And I'm struggling to understand what changed.

I know it's not the stories all over social media.

I know it's not the tape or Amber. He may not love me, but he absolutely doesn't still have feelings for her.

So why would he have turned on me the way he did?

Briar and Aspen have been wonderfully supportive, and though he hasn't said much, I can see that Dash is beyond annoyed with Royal. That's just it, though. They're his *family,* and I would never ask them to make some kind of choice.

Which is why I'm holed up in a hotel suite in Vegas with Lily. She's doing a month-long residency here and it feels like the perfect city to get lost in. She reached out when the sex tape hit the media, and after the break-up, I needed someone to talk to. When she suggested joining her here, I jumped at the chance.

"You okay, sugar?" Lily is tall and lanky, with long black hair and a bright smile. She's been mothering me a bit, which is out of character for her, but I appreciate it.

"No, but I will be." I'm lounging on a chair by the window overlooking the Strip.

"We have to go soon…you gonna change?"

I look down at my jeans and T-shirt. "Nooo…should I?"

She cocks her head. "I was gonna bring you out on stage."

"Oh. No, don't do that. I'm not ready to—"

"You *are* ready. And you need to get your feet back under you before the show at the Opry."

I sigh.

I'd forgotten about the stupid show.

It was booked months ago, and it's a pretty big deal.

Normally, I love performing, but it feels impossible to get out there and put on a show with the way I'm feeling.

"Yeah, I guess." I get up and walk into my bedroom, staring at my suitcase. I didn't bring performance clothes with me, because I had no plans to be on stage.

"I have a top you can borrow," Lily says, standing in the doorway. "The jeans are fine and I know you have boots in there."

I manage a smile. "Yes, of course I do."

"Everything's going to be okay," she says, coming over and sitting on the edge of the bed. "I know it doesn't feel like it, but he has no idea what he's lost. If he treated you this way, you deserve so much better."

"I know all of that intellectually," I mutter, "but my heart doesn't seem to be getting it."

"I met him, you know," she says thoughtfully.

I whirl to face her. "You did? When? Where? Why didn't you tell me?"

"Honestly, I forgot about it. I think it was right before his accident. He performed at the Grammy's…and we wound up at the same after-party. He was there with that she-witch he used to be married to. He was larger than life, but also nice. It's hard to explain. Someone introduced us, and while some of the people I met that night were distant, stuck up, kind of aloof, Royal actually looked at me, said hello, paid attention. It was like, thirty seconds, tops, but I didn't get the vibe that he felt put upon to have to talk to me. And I remember thinking there was more to him than just a spoiled rock star."

"That's just it," I say sadly. "He's a *great* guy. Amazing even. Underneath the bluster and grumpy demeanor is a kind, caring man. He loves his goddaughter to pieces. He's fiercely loyal to his friends and family. He's protective but not overbearing…he ticks all the darn boxes." I take a breath. "*Ticked*. Past tense. Because the way he spoke to me the last time we saw each other is definitely not one of my boxes."

"Did it ever occur to you that he was just lashing out? Like, he literally had no one else to take it out on, and you were just… there?"

"Unacceptable," I say, lifting my chin. "I can't be with a man who thinks he's so much better than me. And, what? He's going to insult me every time we have a fight?"

"Oh, I totally agree with you. I'm just pointing out that it might have simply been a reaction to everything going on. The sex tape, the media coverage, and then finding out he's been replaced in his own band. Not to mention the ex-cunt."

I almost manage another smile. "You're probably right but that doesn't make it any better. We were supposed to be a team, partners, and he turned on me." That's the part that hurts the most. "Look, I don't want to talk about Royal anymore. Find me that top while I put on some makeup."

"You got it."

She leaves the room, and I walk into the bathroom, stare into the mirror.

It feels like I've aged twenty years the last few days. There are dark circles under my eyes because I'm not sleeping, and I've probably lost five or six pounds because I have zero interest in food.

It's kind of pathetic but I know it's a process. I have to grieve the relationship before I can move on, and that's going to take a while.

Because I love the fucking jerk.

I hear Grandma's voice in my head, reprimanding me for being unladylike, but I can't bring myself to care. Not today, anyway.

I've used the word fuck more in the last week than my entire life, and for some reason it feels good. It soothes me in a way nothing else can, and while I don't quite understand it, I'll take whatever relief I can get. Even if it means cursing a blue streak.

I honestly don't want to perform tonight, but Lily is right that it'll be a good way to get ready for the show on Saturday night. I won't get to Nashville until late tomorrow, my band and I will rehearse on Friday, and the show is Saturday. Normally, we would have been rehearsing all week, but the media would find me and I needed time to decompress.

My head is pounding, so I down a couple of aspirin and then dig out my makeup. I truly have no interest in getting dolled up, but it's probably the smart thing to do, so I pull out my concealer and get to work on those dark circles.

My phone buzzes on the counter and I see a text from Briar.

BRIAR: Where are you? Do you want to get together? Aspen and I were thinking dinner and a movie?

JADE: Actually, I'm in Vegas and I leave for Nashville in the morning. The show at the Opry is Saturday and I need a day to rehearse.

BRIAR: How are you doing? Do you need me to fly to Nashville?

JADE: You're sweet to offer, but I'll be okay. I'm lying low with my friend Lily—do not tell anyone!—and then I'm focused on getting through Saturday.

BRIAR: If you change your mind, I can be on the first flight.

JADE: Thank you. You've been a wonderful friend.

BRIAR: Been? That sounds like you're breaking up with me.

JADE: No, of course not. But it's going to be awkward for us to hang out now that Royal and I aren't together. And no matter what you say, or how upset you are with him, you know you still love him.

BRIAR: Yes, of course, but he doesn't get to dictate who my friends are. And I consider you one of them.

JADE: I appreciate that. Truly. Listen, I'm going to perform a few songs with Lily tonight, so I have to get going, but I'll check in once I'm back in Nashville.

BRIAR: You'd better!

JADE: Don't worry, I will. Talk soon.

I put the phone down and go back to my makeup.

"Okay, so I've got the pink corset or the black fringe or the red velvet tank." Lily is standing in the doorway holding up three tops.

I shrug. "You pick."

"You've got a bad case of the blues," she says softly. "I wish I could help."

"The only help for me will be time." I reach for the pink corset she holds up. "And work. The harder I work, the less time I'll have to miss him."

"Okay, then work it is. You want to do 'Forever in Rewind' together? Or is that too much of a reminder of him?"

"No, it's fine." I say the words even though I'm screaming in protest on the inside. "And my fans will expect it on Saturday, so let's do it."

"Done. Now try on these tops while I text the band, let them know we're adding a new song to the set." She's gone before I can say anything, and I rest my hands on the counter, letting my head fall forward.

I'm mentally and physically exhausted, my chest is tight, and I look like death warmed over.

But the first rule in show business is that the show goes on.

No matter what.

Even when the love of your life shatters your world.

Damn you, Royal.

I fight back a fresh wave of tears and slowly lift my head.

I don't know how I'm going to survive this, but I've been through worse.

Somehow, some way, I *will* move forward.

I just don't know who I'll be when I come out the other side.

CHAPTER THIRTY-THREE

Royal

"CHRIST," I growl, tossing my phone onto the island at Briar's house.

I've called in every fucking favor I've had, trying to find out where Jade is, and I've struck out with everything.

And now I see that she's performed a couple of surprise songs in Vegas with Lily Maxwell.

Less than an hour's flight from me, and I can't get there.

Because I'm on babysitting duty.

It's a school night, Atlas and Briar are on a business trip, Aspen is at The Sapphire Room, and Banks is on the road with the Vipers.

Dash is with a client who may or may not be Jade.

And I'm here with Frankie.

Normally something I love.

Uncle time is precious and yet…

I could bring her with me on the plane and be back in time—

Right. Now I'm thinking not only like a pathetic asshole, but also like a bad godfather. I have responsibilities here. I can't just bustle a three-year-old to the City of Sin so I can fix things with Jade.

If I can even fix things.

It hadn't occurred to me until much later.

Fuck you, Royal Ewing.

She cursed at me.

Not that I didn't deserve it. I sure as shit did, and far more.

But *Jade* had cursed.

Not *Frack you, Royal Ewing.* Nor *Screw you, Royal Ewing.* Not even *Fudge you, Royal Ewing.*

Certainly no *Royal Pain-in-the-butt.*

But the full shebang.

And I hate that part of me knows what it represented—I hurt her so deeply that I broke something in her.

I grip the edge of the counter and drop my chin to my chest, my exhale long-suffering.

I'm no good for her.

I should leave her alone.

I should—

No.

I lift my head, reach for my phone again.

I'll find her.

I'll make it up to her. I won't fuck up again.

How, asshole?

It's Colt's voice in my head.

How will you show her that she'll be able to trust you again?

Therapy's a given. I need to stop with this shit, with the anger that makes me lash out at the people I love.

Because Jade's the rule, not the exception. I've hurt Banks and Atlas, Dash and Briar. I've even hurt Frankie. Not with sharp words, but by avoiding her and pulling back and throwing up walls.

And with Jade…

I did *all* of that.

So, I need to figure out my head, need to find a way to let go of…all the negativity.

Yes, my life took a turn. Yes, Amber is knocked up by Tony Blackthorn. Yes, I've been kicked out of the band I founded, that I helped make a success with blood, sweat, and tears.

But I haven't been a part of Midnight Sun, not for a couple of years now, have I?

No.

Not since my accident, since I iced them out beyond anything I wasn't contractually obligated to.

What were they supposed to do? Wait for me forever, when I'll never be what I was?

Should I have heard the news from Amber?

Of fucking course not.

But when is the last time I've taken one of their calls?

I can't remember.

Which…yeah, I fucked up with them too.

Sighing, I scrub my hands over my face.

I have a lot of work to do, too many relationships to fix, a shit-ton of amends to make. It all seems so big that it's overwhelming, that I can feel that insidious panic just beneath the surface.

It would be so easy to sink into it, to let the darkness and pain drag me under.

It's far less scary to be miserable than vulnerable.

My gaze catches on a picture taped to the fridge—the drawing that Frankie did at preschool. It's simple, messy squiggles that form stick people: Frankie, Briar, Atlas, Dash, Aspen, Banks, me and…

Jade.

She's a part of our family.

My family.

And I know that allowing the darkness to swell up and swallow me whole again is untenable.

Because it would mean a life without Jade.

I reach for my phone, and even though I have no way to get to Jade right now, I'm not completely useless. I can take one small step now.

No. *Two.*

The first is less scary than the second and I take the easy route, opening the health network app and typing out a message to my doctor—asking for the referral of physical therapy he's offered at every appointment since the accident.

I don't know if it'll help my hand get any better, if I've truly plateaued, like I've been told, like I've been telling myself.

But I'm going to try, going to put the work in.

I finish the message. Hit send.

Then I'm looking at my list of contacts like a rattlesnake is going to jump out and sink its fangs into me.

Because the next step is harder.

And even though I have the number programmed into my phone, this isn't like physical therapy, tried and put aside in frustration and rage when no further progress seemed to be in sight. This is…

Vulnerable and dark all over again.

This is pulling myself into the light.

I've never called the number, not even when the guys all but threatened to tie me up and drag me to the grief counselor's office. But I did accept Atlas's compromise of having it saved into my contacts in case I ever felt the need to use it.

Funny that it's been years now.

And it's taken until now to finally be ready to make the call.

I tap my finger against the screen, bring my phone to my ear, and listen to it ring. Once. Twice. Three times.

I'm mentally preparing my voicemail when the brusque feminine voice comes on the line.

"This is Catherine."

"I—" But the words stopper up in my throat, and I find that I suddenly don't know what to say.

I'm a fuck up. Please help?

"Hello?"

There's a rustling sound, as though she's going to hang up, and my throat loosens.

"Wait!"

"This is Catherine Wells. Who am I speaking to?"

Christ, why is this hard?

"R-Royal Ewing," I finally manage to get out. "Atlas Delarosa gave me your number. I thought..." I lose my words again because I'm not sure what to say...*I thought you might be able to fix me?* That's—

Ugh.

It's exposed, dangerous. *Pathetic.*

Jade's hurt gray eyes flash into my mind.

No. I owe it to Jade.

To myself.

It's the only way I can be a good enough man to trust that I won't hurt her again.

I exhale, not missing that Catherine isn't pushing me to finish the thought, just patiently waiting. "My mind isn't in a good place. I'm struggling, and I've lashed out, hurt the people I love too many times." Then I realize how that sounds, feel compelled to add, "Not physically, just..."

This time she does finish for me.

"With words?"

"Yes," I rasp.

"Okay then." A slight pause, which isn't the worst thing considering that the no nonsense words leaves me reeling for a moment. "I can do a virtual appointment late tonight. Or if you prefer in person I can see you Monday or Tuesday of next week."

Tonight is terrifying.

But...

It *needs* to be tonight.

I need to start now.

"I can do tonight," I say, my voice still hoarse. "I'm babysitting my niece but she'll be in bed by eight."

A pause, and maybe I'm imaging it, but I feel approval coming through the airwaves.

A delusion, likely.

Still, I'm taking it.

"Great. We'll meet at eight-thirty. I'll text a secure virtual meeting link to this number. You'll put in a payment method. My rates are…"

I stay on the line for the next couple of minutes, listening to her rate card, her cancelation policy, how to reach her in the case of an emergency, and the information buzzes around my mind as she says goodbye and hangs up before I can reply.

She's…

Well…*brusque*.

Brusque may be a strange trait for a therapist, and yet, I know that if she was gentle or soft or sweet, I wouldn't have been able to go through with this.

I need someone to match the jagged edges of me, someone who's protected and not going to get wounded by my bullshit.

Someone who'll push me so I can push myself.

That's not my family's job.

That's not Jade's either.

I need them to love me, and I'll love them back.

I need *her* to love me, and I'll give her the world.

I just…

Have to get to her first.

I exhale, rubbing the ache in my chest as I hear footsteps pound down the hall, signaling that Frankie's daily love affair with Ms. Rachel has ended.

"Time for dinner, Tater Tot?" I ask as she runs into the kitchen.

"I want dino nuggets!"

I grin, despite myself. Her enthusiasm and brightness are impossible to not take to heart.

"Then you get dino nuggets." I shoot her a look. "And carrots."

Her nose wrinkles.

"Because we need veggies *and* because we need sharp eyesight so we can see the right notes to play."

"Do carrots do that?"

I tug a strand of her hair, even though I don't know if that's true or just an old wives' tale. "They sure do."

"Okay! Can we have apples too?"

"With peanut butter?"

She nods so vigorously she resembles a bobblehead. "Yup."

"Then definitely."

It's not until a half hour later, when we're chowing down on carrots, apples and peanut butter, and those required dino nuggets smothered with plenty of ranch, that I get my first big break in my quest to get close to Jade.

And I can't help but think that the universe is rewarding me for finally pulling my head out of my ass.

"Are you going with Auntie Jade to the Opera show?" Frankie asks, licking ranch off one finger.

I frown, ignore the pulse of pain at Jade's name, and try to decipher that.

"What show, Tater Tot?" I ask.

"The Opera one," she repeats, screwing up her face in concentration. "Mommy and Auntie Aspen were talking about a Grand Opera show that Auntie Jade has soon." Her eyes come back to mine.

Grand Opera.

Grand…

The pieces slide into place.

The Grand *Ole Opry*.

Jade has a show there? Holy shit, that's big. That's *amazing*.

That's…

Where she will be.

"Are you going?" Frankie presses.

I reach for my phone, text the operator of the private jet service I use, and then I meet Frankie's eyes.

"Yeah, Tater Tot. I'm going."

CHAPTER THIRTY-FOUR

Jade

"You're lookin' a little peaked there, sugarplum." My longtime makeup artist, Fannie Mason, meets my gaze in the mirror.

"It's been a rough week," I admit.

"Yeah, sex tapes will do that to you." She shakes her head but it's not with censure. "The media just loves that type of crap. But don't worry—someone else will do something a lot worse any minute now, and they'll forget all about you. I mean, that Tony Blackthorn's wedding is all anybody's talking about now…"

Ew.

Tony Blackthorn.

The guy Amber is marrying.

The one replacing Royal in his band.

Yuck. I don't want to think about them so I tune out Fannie's rambling, talking about who got Botox, who wants a facelift, and who's rumored to be here tonight.

I don't really care about any of it.

I go on stage in an hour and whereas I don't get much stage fright anymore, there's usually a little bit of jittery anxiety before a big show like this. Tonight, I feel nothing. No fear, no anxiety, no excitement—a big, fat nothing.

God, this sucks.

I've never experienced this kind of sadness—missing someone so much it's often hard to breathe. How on earth am I going to get through a two-hour set? My plan to work Royal out of my system appears to be failing miserably.

"Now you look like your usual million-dollar self!" Fannie says, turning my chair so I can see the final product.

And I do look pretty damn good. Even if I *feel* like shit.

"Thank you, Fannie. You're amazing." I squeeze her arm as I slide out of the chair.

"I'll be in the wings if you need any touch-ups mid-set!" she says as she heads for the door.

"Thank you!" I close the door behind her and lean against it.

Time to get dressed and put on my game face.

So to speak.

My phone buzzes and I smile at the text that just came in.

BRIAR: Kick ass and take names! And Frankie sent you this:

She attached a video so I press the little arrow to play it.

It's of Frankie, playing guitar.

And singing an incredibly off-key version of "Forever in Rewind."

It's so sweet it brings tears to my eyes.

But I take a deep breath so Fannie doesn't kill me for ruining my makeup.

JADE: Tell her the next time I play in L.A., she can come on stage with me.

BRIAR: Oh, God, I can't tell her that—she'll never stop talking about it!

JADE: LOL Well, then tell her she did an amazing job and almost made me cry.

BRIAR: You doing okay?

JADE: I'm fine, gotta go! Thanks for checking in.

I change into fishnet stockings, a denim miniskirt, and a black leather vest that laces up the front. I'm usually a little more modest on stage, but I've decided I hate that look. It was fun wearing something sexy up on stage with Lily, so I'm going to do it tonight. If Carrie Underwood can look hotter than the surface of Mars and sell a zillion records, then so can I.

I slide on my favorite red airbrushed cowboy boots and take a few minutes to breathe.

In through my nose.

Out through my mouth.

A soft knock on the door. "Jade? You ready?"

"Two minutes!" I call.

This is it.

I rub my hands down my skirt and roll my neck, hoping to relax a little. I'm not nervous, but I'm tense. It's all in my head, from the emotion and heartbreak I've dealt with this week, but I'll be fine once I get on stage.

I open my dressing room door, and my two new security guards—thank you, Dash—are waiting to walk me down the hall that leads to the stage.

"Nashville, are you ready for Jade Cantrell?" The announcement over the public address system gets the crowd roaring.

The venue is sold out, and I take a moment to send a little prayer up into the ether to Grandma Louise, Mama, and Daddy. I do it before every show. It's not a religious thing so much as a habit. Something I've done since my very first performance in high school.

The lights go down and I walk out on stage.

"Nashville! I'm home!"

The crowd goes wild as a single spotlight focuses on me.

"Did y'all miss me?" I ask, wrapping my hand around the microphone.

Another round of shouting and cheers.

The band breaks into one of my earliest hits, a song called "Happy Tuesday." The audience sings along and for a little while, I forget everything.

This is my happy place.

This is where I'm not alone.

This is everything.

We play three songs without a break and then I pause to guzzle some water.

"Oooh, it's hot in here tonight," I say. "Are we ready to slow things down?"

I wait for the familiar piano intro but it doesn't come. The crowd is hooting and whistling, and I glance over my shoulder to see what Eli, my keyboard player, is doing.

And he's not there.

What the hell?

I gaze into the wings just as a familiar—but very unplanned —melody starts up.

Goose bumps crawl over my skin and my heart skips a beat.

How is this happening?

What is happening?

I whirl to find out what's going on.

"Hey, Nashville—how are we doing tonight?"

My mind is racing, unable to comprehend what's happening..

"My name is Royal Ewing, and I'm here to ask you for a special favor…"

Royal?

Royal!

What on earth…

I gape as the most beautiful man I've ever seen strides out on stage, my acoustic guitar in his left hand.

The crowd knows who he is, and it's like an explosion of cheering and catcalls as he walks across the stage like he owns it.

"I need your help tonight," he continues. "You see, I kind of messed up with my girl, and I need to make it right. Do you think you can help me?"

The audience is on their feet, hands in the air, shouting encouragement and God only knows what else.

"This woman right here—" He points to me and our eyes meet for the first time.

His are warm and filled with myriad emotions. Worry, fear, regret…*and hope.* There's no doubt about that. I just don't understand what's going on.

"—she's the best thing to ever happen to me. And we had a disagreement. Totally my fault because I'm kind of a grumpy SOB. But I love her more than life itself. Her talent, her sweet soul, her giant heart—everything about her. So I need you guys to help convince her to forgive me." He puts the guitar on a stand and then, as I stand there with my mouth open, drops to one knee.

He's holding something out but I can't focus through the tears blurring my vision.

The crowd is screaming, "Say yes. Say yes. Say yes!"

"Royal?" I whisper his name, and though I'm sure he can't hear me over the noise, he sees my lips move.

"I'm right here, baby."

"I don't…" I take a step toward him. "What are you—"

"Say yes. Say yes. Say yes!"

"Marry me," he says, moving his microphone to the side so he's using his regular voice. "And I'll spend the rest of my life making the last week up to you. I love you, Jade, and don't want to spend another minute without you."

"Say yes! Say yes! Say yes!"

"Royal." I cover my mouth with my hand, fighting so many emotions.

"Say yes! Say yes! Say yes!"

I want to say no, but I can't quite bring myself to.

"Will you marry me?" he whispers against my mouth, his lips finding mine.

And I'm helpless to resist.

The crowd is on their feet, yelling and cheering as we kiss. And kiss. And kiss some more.

Then he's up, sliding a ring on my finger and his arm around my waist.

It sounds like all four thousand people in attendance are screaming at the top of their lungs. I'm still a little shell shocked, but Royal's next to me, his body warm against mine.

He looks down at me, his eyes filled with something I've never seen before.

Is that what love looks like?

I don't know, and we don't have time to talk.

"Ready?" he asks.

I'm not ready for any of this. "For what?"

"To play 'Midnight Snow.'"

"The band doesn't know it…"

"They do. I might've sent them the tape earlier today." His smile is impish. "If not, you and I can handle it."

There might be some double meaning in that statement.

"But…" I want to protest. I don't play a lot of guitar live, but I can.

I will.

For him.

With him.

I unstick, put my performer hat back on and ask the crowd, "Who wants to hear our new single?" They roar before I go on. "It's called 'Midnight Snow,' and it's coming out on Valentine's Day."

Someone brings over two stools and my acoustic, and I sit, Royal beside me.

I gaze over at him, and for the briefest moment, it's just the two of us.

Back in the cabin.

In the studio.

In his living room.

At Sunday dinner.

The magic is still there and the music is like a physical presence when we're together, making it almost tangible.

He's waiting.

The crowd is waiting.

And there's no doubt what I'm going to do.

I smile, my fingers moving into position easily.

The opening notes fill the venue.

Midnight," Royal starts the vocals, his voice deep and rich. *"When there's no one but you and me, girl. Snowfall, like an avalanche of pearls. Come and show me…"*

And I join in.

There's no time like midnight when it's snowing
I look in your eyes, baby, you're glowing
Show me the moon and I'll give you the stars
Baby, you know me, and this night is ours.

CHAPTER THIRTY-FIVE

Royal

I'm sitting in the green room, watching the monitor as Jade finishes up the last of her songs, the planned encore, and then another, unplanned, one.

She's fucking magnificent.

A total natural who lights up the stage, and the crowd is on fire for her.

And, yes, I'm considering myself part of the crowd.

I'm burning for her, trying to get a handle on this insatiable need to draw her close again, to tell her all the apologies I've been crafting over the last week, to make all the promises I owe her, to start showing her I know exactly what the fuck I nearly lost and that I will never—fucking *never*—take her for granted again.

But with every moment that passes, the doubt is creeping in.

And it sure as shit doesn't help that she seems to be doing her level best to make this show as long as fucking possible.

The crowd roars, and I hear her call, "Goodnight, Nashville!" before she turns and walks off the stage.

The feed cuts, and I jump up from the couch, nervous energy

making my movements jerky. I pace as I wait, fully aware of the panic eating at my insides. Is she going to be pissed that I stormed in and took over her show—even if it was just for one song? Is she going to forgive me?

I close my eyes, practice the breathing that Catherine helped me with last night.

Jade accepted the ring.

She didn't call security to haul my ass off stage.

She stayed close as we played our song, our hands working together on the guitar in perfect harmony.

For those three minutes and twenty-two seconds, the crowd faded away. It became Jade and me up in the mountains, the snow falling, the fire roaring, the song flowing out of us like the most effortless sort of breathing.

And then I kissed her, whispered that I love her, and let her have the rest of her moment.

It was perfect, exactly as I imagined it would be…

But what if it's not enough?

I wait in the now silent green room for what feels like ages before the door slowly opens and one of Dash's security guard pokes his head in, eyes sweeping suspiciously over the space. They linger on me, his expression inscrutable, and he must determine that I'm not a threat because he moves forward, pushing the door open with him, stepping to the side, allowing…

My heart to walk through the door.

Jade's face glistens with sweat and she has a towel hanging around her shoulders.

Her color is high, her hair a mess, that outfit beyond fucking sexy.

And she's so beautiful that I can't breathe.

But it's her eyes that plunge a knife in my belly, tearing my flesh.

Fuck.

It wasn't enough.

I move to her, reach for her hands, hating when she skitters back a step. "Shortcake," I murmur. "I—"

She turns to the security guard. "Trent," she says softly. "Will you give me some privacy?"

He nods at her, but gives me a long, lingering glare that silently threatens to dismember me if I so much as harm a hair on her head. He can't know that I wouldn't hurt her that way, can't know that the wounds I've already inflicted are far more damaging.

Or maybe he does.

Because his blue eyes turn to ice and he tells Jade, "I'll be right outside if you need *anything*."

Anything meaning giving me concrete shoes and taking me for a swim in a deep lake.

Or skydiving without a parachute.

Or—

Right.

I'm delaying.

"Shortcake," I say again, stepping toward her.

She puts up her hand, my ring glinting on her finger, and fuck if I don't feel a hundred feet tall when I see it there.

Mine.

At least until she starts talking.

Then a giant boulder sits on my stomach.

"I wasn't going to embarrass you on stage," she says, "but you can't possibly think that I'm going to forgive you just because you bought a ring."

"It's not just a ring, baby. I…" My throat works, panic edging in, that streak of vulnerable far too wide for my comfort.

I shove it down.

Because I need to make this right.

"I had a week without you and it's been the worst one in of my life—worse than losing Colt, worse than waking up after the accident, definitely worse that Amber telling me she was leaving, and a fuck-ton worse than finding out I've been replaced in

Midnight Sun." I reach for her, relief sliding through me when she allows me to take her hands in mine.

"I'm sorry they did that," she murmurs. "And did it that way."

"That doesn't matter. I—"

"It matters, Royal," she says firmly.

Because of what I did afterward.

Guilt churns but I push it down. I need to focus. So, I exhale silently and ask, "Please, just let me talk, baby?"

She nods, and I draw her slowly toward me, inch by careful inch, trying not to spook her, not stopping until she's flush against me, the jagged pit that's been in my stomach for the last week filling in, just a little bit.

"First, I am so sorry. Hearing it like that—" I close my eyes, push out a breath, then open them again. "It hit me hard, Shortcake, and I fucked up. I went to that place again, the one that hurts everyone I love—"

She jerks.

But I keep talking.

"I need you to know that I'm not going to let that happen again—"

"Royal—"

"I finally talked to a therapist that Atlas recommended years ago, and I'm going to keep seeing her. I need to get a handle on the anger, the grief, the panic that closes in on me at the thought of not being what I was—"

She jerks again. *"Royal."*

"I know that I probably won't ever get back to being that man again, but I'm going to try. I made an appointment with my physical therapist, and I won't give up this time—not until they tell me there's no hope. Fuck, I won't give up even then." I touch her cheek. "I'm going to be better, I promise."

"Honey," she whispers.

But I still don't stop.

"And I didn't mean that bullshit about your music." I settle my other hand on her cheek, holding her stare so she knows that I'm serious. "You are so fucking talented, baby. The first time I saw you on stage, I knew you had it—that star power that only comes with musicians who change the industry, who are around their whole lives and continue making hit after hit, whose music touches people's souls. *You're* one of those, Shortcake. Your fans will be around for a lifetime and your music is going to change lives—"

"*Our* music."

My heart flips over in my chest. "What?"

"*Our* music is going to change the industry, change lives, and touch people's souls."

That tightness in my lungs isn't panic for once.

"I just have one question."

"Anything."

Her gray eyes are warm. "How much of yourself are you willing to give me?"

I don't have to think about it, not even for a second. "You already have all of me, Shortcake."

"Right," she says, her eyes warming further. "Now go back to what you were saying before."

"About physical therapy?"

Her face gentles. "That's really good, baby. I'm glad you're going to go. But no"—she shakes her head—"not about that."

"About my other therapy?"

Her hand—her *left*—hand covers mine. "That's also wonderful, baby. But no, not that either."

"That I'm not going to let it happen again?"

"Also, good. And"—her gentle eyes fill with steel-like determination—"something that I require because the way you talked to me can never—fucking *never*—happen again." A beat. "But not that either."

My stomach twists. "About the cursing?"

"No. It turns out that fuck and fiddlesticks both have their uses." She smiles. "But no, go further back."

I wrack my mind for what I'd said.

Then freeze.

"Yeah," she whispers. "*That.*"

"I love you?"

"That's twice now you've said it," she murmurs.

"And twice now I've meant it more than life itself."

She inhales sharply. "*Royal.*"

"I love you so fucking much, baby, and I will spend the rest of my days making up for this week if you'll only forgive me."

Those storm cloud gray eyes lock onto mine, her mouth curving into a rueful half-smile. "I think—even though I was desperate to hold a grudge—I forgave you days ago." Her body drifts forward, presses forward to rest fully against me. "I love you, Royal."

"Baby—"

"But I need to make it clear," she says.

"Anything, Shortcake."

Her gaze pierces into mine. "I meant what I said before. You cannot *ever* treat me that way again. It doesn't matter how much I love you, I can't be with a person who does that."

"I understand."

She holds my stare for long moments.

Long enough that the panic takes a swipe at me again.

But then she says the best thing ever. "Okay, then."

Relief rushes through me, and I drag her even closer, slanting my mouth over hers, pouring in every bit of that emotion, every bit of love, every bit of need into the kiss.

When we break apart we're both breathing hard.

I settle my forehead against hers. "I'm—"

"No more apologies." She settles her hand on my chest, just above my heart. "Just actions." Her mouth tips up. "Kind of like tonight's big one."

"Is that—was that okay?"

Her brows drag together. "What do you mean?"

"It was your big show and I—" My cheeks get warm. "I kind of took over."

Her fingers flex, lips curving. "That was the biggest gift you could have given me," she murmurs. "I know how much it took for you to do it, how much you hate being in the public eye like that. It wasn't just a song or playing a show—though 'Midnight Snow' *killed*—it was baring your soul, owning up to a mistake in front of thousands of people."

"So..." My throat works. "It was okay?"

"It was about as perfect of an apology as you could have given me." She grins. "In fact, how are you possibly going to top this the next time you screw up?"

I still and then start laughing.

And the best part is that she does too.

"Don't worry, Shortcake, I've got plenty of ideas."

Her hand begins sliding down my chest. "Know what?"

"What?"

"I have plenty of *ideas* too."

Heat begins blooming in my belly, arrowing further south. "Yeah? What kind of *ideas?*"

Her cheeks go pink, but she lifts on tiptoe, mouth going to my ear as she whispers...

My dick goes hard. "Holy fuck, where'd you get a mouth like that, baby?"

Her grin widens, and her stormy gray eyes spark with lightning. "Mmm." She drops back onto her heels and moves to the door, flicking the lock. "I'd like to think I learned from the best. Now"—her boots click on the floor as she closes the distance between us, takes my hand, and draws me to the couch on the far side of the room—"it's time."

"Time for what?" I rasp as she clambers into my lap.

"Time to write the music of the rest of our lives."

EPILOGUE

Jade

IT'S RELEASE DAY.

Valentine's Day.

Just like we planned.

I'm up early, despite how late we'd been up last night, and I slide out of bed quietly. I love cuddling with Royal in the morning—and what that usually leads to—but today I need a moment to myself.

"Midnight Snow" released at midnight.

We celebrated with a bottle of champagne and then made love in the sun room, a blanket of stars all around us.

It's certainly too early to know how the song is going to do, but my release days tend to follow a pattern: big jump just after midnight, a lull in the morning, and then a bigger jump around dinnertime. I don't have access to real-time sales numbers at this stage, but I can look at the charts.

I open my phone and—

Tears fill my eyes.

Number one.

Number one on Apple.

Number one on Spotify.

Four million views on YouTube.

"Baby?" Royal's sleep-addled voice startles me, and I turn as the first tear slides down my cheek.

"What's wrong?" he asks in alarm, immediately reaching for me.

"Look!" I hand him my phone, and it takes a second for him to digest what he's looking at.

Then a slow, appreciative smile crosses his face. "Well, look at that. You did it."

"*We* did it," I whisper, moving into his arms.

"Why are you crying?"

"Because I'm so happy."

He chuckles, lowering his head to lightly kiss me. "But why did you sneak out of bed?"

"Because…" I worry my lower lip.

How can I explain it?

"Babe?" His eyes are filled with patient curiosity.

"Well, I was afraid."

"Of me?" His eyes widen in alarm.

"No, no, of course not." I wind my arms around his neck. "Never. Not like that. But I was afraid that the song might not be doing well and you'd be…disappointed."

He frowns. "Disappointed in what way? Disappointed that it's not the hit we thought it would be? Maybe I would have been—a little bit anyway. But you didn't think I'd be disappointed in you…did you?"

I drop my gaze. "Maybe?"

"Hey. Look at me." He pulls me closer. "That's never going to happen. Do you hear me? We both know how fickle this industry is. Sometimes it's about timing. Something going on in politics. An earthquake in the South Pacific. Anything and everything can impact the performance of a release. But there is no universe, no set of circumstances, where I could be disappointed in *you*. Especially not with this particular song. Baby, we put our souls into 'Midnight Snow.' Nothing diminishes that. Or how I feel about you."

I rest my head against his chest and close my eyes.

This is my safe place.

My happy place.

The only place I want to be ninety-nine percent of the time.

"I love you," I whisper.

"I love you too, Shortcake." He gently runs his hands up and down my back. *Both* hands. With equal pressure.

The fingers on his right hand are still a long way from doing what they used to do, but his new physical therapist is teaching him different ways to use his entire hand to compensate for some of the loss of control. He also firmly believes Royal will play guitar again. Not at the same level, but enough to write music, maybe perform a few songs with me when we go on tour.

It's the first and only time I've ever seen tears in Royal's eyes.

"Let's go back to bed," I say after a moment.

"Need a little cock to celebrate being number one?" he teases.

I snort out a laugh. "Yes, you animal."

"You like my animalistic tendencies." He waggles his brows then suddenly lifts me off the floor, tossing me over his shoulder.

"Royal!" I let out a pretend shriek of indignance and he slaps my ass.

"Bed or shower?" he asks.

"Bed."

"You got it." He dumps me on the mattress, landing on top of me after quickly shedding his boxers. "Now, tell me again why you were crying…"

I smile. "Tears of joy, my love. Tears of joy."

He kisses them away. "Now how about we make tears of pleasure?"

My smile grows.

Because he proceeds to do just that.

And as usual, the music we make together is perfect.

"I'M SO sorry I'm not there." Royal's voice is filled with apology.

Considering this is at least the fourth time he's apologized, I can't help but smile.

It's a week later and I'm in Dallas, while he's still back in L.A.

"Babe, it's okay. Frankie needs you. I'll be fine. Dash is here, and I'll be on the first flight back to L.A. tomorrow morning."

"I just wanted to be there."

"There's always next time. You take care of Frankie and I'll be back before you know it."

"I love you."

"I love you too. Kiss that baby girl for me."

"I will."

I disconnect and sigh.

Atlas and Briar are in Shanghai on a business trip. Royal and I were staying at the house with Frankie, and all three of us were going to come to Dallas for the new MCM award show—Modern Country Music. Except Frankie came home from school with RSV and is sick as a dog. Banks is on a road trip, Aspen can't help out because she can't risk getting sick, and when it came down to whether Dash or Royal would come with me, we decided Dash was the better option.

I trust Trent, who's become my new head of security, but his girlfriend just had a baby so he's on paternity leave. Which left Dash as the person I trust most with my safety.

So Royal stayed home, and Dash and I are here in Dallas.

I'm not upset—poor Frankie has been miserable—but I miss Royal.

We haven't been apart since we got engaged, and it was really strange sleeping alone last night.

"You ready, Jade?" Dash looks incredibly handsome in his tuxedo, and I go over to straighten his collar. Tuxes are a requirement for security at this event, and he'd grumbled about it, but I think it's a great look for him. Those broad shoulders will turn quite a few heads this evening…but he's all business.

So much so, sometimes I worry about him.

He needs a good woman to ease the perpetual frown line between his brows. Aside from his time at The Sapphire Room, he's always worried. On alert. *Working*. Frankly, it's exhausting just to watch.

Part of me feels guilty because he's my friend more than my bodyguard now, and I reap the rewards of his expertise, but I also want him to be happy. And deep down, I think he's just as alone as Royal was. Him and Atlas both. Atlas is a much tougher nut to crack, though.

And I'm certainly not playing matchmaker tonight.

I'm up for Country Music Superstar of the Year, and it's a little strange since this is a newer award. This is only the second year this event has been happening, and this year it's on all the major prime-time television stations.

I smooth down my raspberry red gown and get ready to leave. Dash is both my date and my bodyguard for the evening, so he'll be with me the whole time. Lots of celebrities do it this way if they don't have an actual date, but I'm sure the gossip mongers will be confused.

That just makes me laugh.

Royal and I have begun to enjoy screwing with the press.

"You look lovely," Dash says as we head for the limo.

"Thank you." I take his arm as we walk. "You look pretty handsome yourself. You know, I bet you'd like my friend Lily. We're going to see her later."

He chuckles. "Stop with the matchmaking. I'm not looking."

"How come?"

"Because I don't have the time. Or the energy. Women are a lot of work."

"What are you trying to say?" I demand, laughing. "Are you calling me high-maintenance?"

He wobbles his hand from side to side. "A little?"

"Well, I never!" I laugh, and he does too.

Conversation is light on the short drive to the event and thankfully, there's no red carpet tonight. But the convention center is literally surrounded by fans and paparazzi.

"Jesus, it's packed," I murmur as we make our way inside.

"Don't worry. I'm right here." He allows me to walk ahead of him, and I wave to a handful of photographers I know, breezing past them to our seats.

"I think you're going to win," he says quietly, looking around.

I cock my head. "Why?"

"I don't know. Just a feeling I have."

"You seem like you're on edge," I say. "Everything okay?"

"Sometimes I just get a vibe—like something is going to happen. I don't always know if it's good or bad, but it's like a sixth sense."

"Well, then let's assume you're right that I'm going to win!" I say. "Because we don't want anything bad to happen."

"Definitely not."

There's that scowl again.

ROYAL: Good luck, Shortcake. Frankie and I will be watching!

JADE: Thank you. I love you.

ROYAL: I love you too.

I put my phone away and try to focus on the emcee, the entertainment, the other awards. Country Music Superstar of the Year will be last, of course, which means I can't even take a bathroom break.

And finally, it's time.

I won't be overly disappointed if I don't win.

It's a new award, new organization within the music industry, new everything, so it doesn't hold a lot of weight yet.

But it would still be cool.

"And the winner is…"

There's the typical dramatic pause, and it takes a lot of self-control not to grab Dash's hand.

"...Jade Cantrell!"

"There you go." Dash smiles triumphantly.

I stand up and he gently squeezes my hand.

I don't even have a speech planned because I didn't want to assume anything.

Now I'm going to have to come up with one on the fly.

"Thank you, Dallas!" I say after accepting the small but heavy glass award in the shape of a cowboy hat. "I'm so honored to win this. First and foremost, thank you to Grandma Louise and my Mama, who instilled the love of music in me."

Lots of cheering and clapping.

"And to my amazing fiancé, Royal Ewing, who couldn't be here tonight—I love you. Oh! And feel better, Frankie!" No one knows who I'm talking about, but I don't give a damn. "The last year has been incredibly chaotic. In the best possible way. Awards like this mean everything…I appreciate my fans, my team, and all of you—my contemporaries. Thank you!" I raise my hand, holding the glass award as the music comes up and I start to exit the stage.

But something in my peripheral vision catches my eye.

Instinctively, I step back as a man lunges onto the stage and comes at me.

Startled, I drop the award and it shatters as it hits the ground.

"Stupid cunt! You don't deserve shit!"

I shrink back, unsure what to do, and then like an arrow shooting through the night, Dash is there. He puts himself between me and my attacker, and I see the glint of metal.

"Dash—he has a knife!"

Dash is still between us, his large body a barrier that's both soothing and terrifying because I can't see what's happening.

"Sugar, let's get you out of here and let security handle it."

One of the announcers comes to my side, putting her arm around me.

But I can't leave Dash.

Not when he's in danger because of me.

It's ridiculous, since I know he can take care of himself, but I look back over my shoulder as I'm forcibly propelled backstage.

More security has descended on the stage but not before my attacker lunges at Dash.

I can only see a tiny bit of their scuffle.

And then both of them go careening off the stage.

"Dash!" I scream his name and hurry back in that direction.

"Jade!" Someone is trying to stop me, but there's a melee on the floor in front of the stage. Security guards everywhere, police, yelling, the sound of breaking glass.

I can't see anything, but when it's all over, an officer has my attacker in handcuffs.

And I still don't see Dash.

"Dash?" I run forward, oblivious to the people trying to pull me back. "Dash! Where is my bodyguard?!" I demand.

A police officer approaches me, a serious look on his face.

"Ms. Cantrell, we've called for paramedics."

"Where. Is. Dash?" I try to see around him but he's blocking me.

"Ms. Cantrell, I don't think—"

"Tell me what happened!" I snap, losing my patience.

I see paramedics surrounding someone on the floor.

"...could be a spinal injury…"

"Get the backboard…"

"Don't move him…"

My hands fly to my mouth.

"Oh, my God."

"Jade." Lily appears at my side. I'd known she was going to be here and we'd made plans to meet up for a late dinner. She slides an arm around my waist. "Come on—come with me. We can follow them to the hospital. I've got security and you can't be alone."

She's right, but I don't want to leave Dash.

"I have to call…" Who do I call first? Royal? Atlas? *Briar?*

"Let's go to my limo. Come on, honey. Let them take care of him."

Tears sting my eyelids as she gets the pertinent information from the paramedics about where they're taking him.

The moment we're in her limo, I call Royal.

"Hey, baby! Congratulations!"

They must have cut to a commercial.

He must not have seen.

"Royal!" I burst into tears.

"Shortcake, what's wrong?"

"It's Dash—he's been hurt. And I think it's bad."

GAMEBREAKERS

Icebreaker
Heartbreaker
Dealbreaker
Rulebreaker
Oathbreaker

ABOUT THE AUTHORS

USA Today bestselling author, Elise Faber, loves chocolate, Star Wars, Harry Potter, and hockey (the order depending on the day and how well her team — the Sharks! — are playing). She and her husband also play as much hockey as they can squeeze into their schedules, so much so that their typical date night is spent on the ice. Elise is the mom to two exuberant boys and lives in Northern California. Connect with her in her Facebook group, the Fabinators or find more information about her books at www.elisefaber.com.

facebook.com/elisefaberauthor
amazon.com/author/elisefaber
bookbub.com/profile/elise-faber
instagram.com/elisefaber
tiktok.com/@elisefaberauthor
goodreads.com/elisefaber
patreon.com/EliseFaber

ABOUT THE AUTHORS

USA Today Bestselling author Kat Mizera was born in Miami Beach with a healthy dose of wanderlust. She's lived from coast to coast, and everywhere in between, but home is wherever her family is.

A devoted mom and wife to her wonderful and supportive husband (Kevin) and two amazing boys (Nick and Max), Kat loves to travel the globe with her adventurous, hockey loving family. Greece is at the top of that list. She hopes to one day retire there, spending her days writing books on the beach.

Kat is former freelance sports writer who now writes steamy hockey romance about her favorite fictional teams, the Las Vegas Sidewinders and the Alaska Blizzard. The library of novels she's penned also include sexy contemporary stories about baseball stars, alpha sex club owners, special forces heroes, rock stars and royalty. Regardless of genre, her books about bad boys with hearts of gold will steal your breath, rock your world and melt your heart.

WHERE TO FOLLOW KAT:
www.katmizera.com
Kat's Private Facebook Group
https://bit.ly/KatMizeraFBGroup

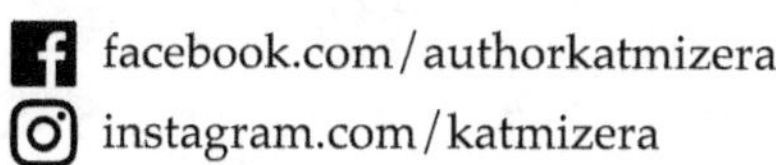

www.ingramcontent.com/pod-product-compliance
Lightning Source LLC
LaVergne TN
LVHW010607100826
845148LV00014B/2877

* 9 7 8 1 6 3 7 4 9 1 4 5 4 *